Seduced
BY THE HEIR

Pamela Yaye

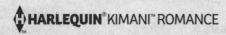
HARLEQUIN® KIMANI™ ROMANCE

I wouldn't be a multipublished author without my amazing critique
partners, Donna Tunney and Leica Cornwall (of Avon books).
I can't imagine not having you lovely ladies in my life and
feel incredibly blessed to call you my friends. I appreciate your
encouragement, your unwavering support and your honesty.
Next time we meet at BP for lunch, it's on me! :)

Recycling programs
for this product may
not exist in your area.

ISBN-13: 978-0-373-86369-3

SEDUCED BY THE HEIR

For questions and comments about the quality of this book please contact us
at CustomerService@Harlequin.com.

Printed in U.S.A.

www.Harlequin.com

Dear Reader,

Rafael Morretti, the firstborn of Arturo and Vivica Morretti, embodies all the traits of an oldest child. He's a born leader with a high IQ who'd much rather work than party. But when he travels to Venice, Italy, for his best friend's wedding and comes face-to-face with his old college sweetheart, Paris St. Clair, he steps up his game and pours on the charm! Being with Paris is so easy, so natural, and their chemistry is stronger than ever. The couple spend a magical weekend together exploring tourist hot spots, dining in posh restaurants and slow dancing under the stars. And after an explosive night of lovemaking on New Year's Eve, Rafael feels himself falling fast….

I LOVE the Morretti family and hope to write about this dynamic, close-knit clan for many more years to come. If you keep reading, I promise to keep writing! :)

I'm anxiously waiting to "hear" what you think of Rafael and Paris's sizzling love story, so drop me a line at pamelayaye@aol.com, find me on Facebook or visit my website, www.pamelayaye.com.

Thanks for the support. Happy reading, and be blessed.

With love,

Pamela Yaye

Chapter 1

"I've wanted to meet you for years, and it looks like today is my lucky day!"

Like a genie in a bottle, a voluptuous woman in a gold strapless dress appeared at Rafael Morretti's side, flashing a seductive smile. He had been searching the tent for his friend Stefano Via, but couldn't find the gregarious stockbroker anywhere. Stefano and his bride-to-be, Cassandra Knight, had rented the lavish countryside villa, near Venice, Italy, for their week-long wedding celebration. And the three-hundred-plus guests inside the satin-draped tent were partying like there was no tomorrow. Conversation was loud and boisterous, the live band was whipping the fashionably dressed crowd into a frenzy, and the mood was energetic and festive.

"I spotted you the moment you arrived." A girlish giggle fell from between her thin, peach lips. "Being over six feet tall, *and* drop-dead gorgeous makes you kinda hard to miss."

Raising an eyebrow, Rafael regarded his female admirer closely. The blue-eyed temptress didn't seem to care about sending the wrong impression or offending the other guests. In fact, she was determined to violate his personal space, and to rub her body against his. *Damn,* he thought, searching the tent for an escape route. *Now I know how a waitress feels during happy hour!*

"I'm a huge fan of your work, and I have every magazine you've ever been featured in."

Rafael raised his glass to his mouth and tasted his Dom
Perignon. The blonde was staring at him with adoration,
as if he was a rock star and she was his number one fan.
But Rafael wasn't moved by her sultry tone or her provocative pout. Her blatant come-on was a turnoff. Call him old-
fashioned, but he didn't like the aggressive, take-charge
types. He preferred classy, refined women who carried
themselves with grace and dignity. *A huge fan of my work?*
he thought, puzzled by her words. *Can't say I've ever heard*
that *line before. I hope she doesn't think I'm Emilio.*

His younger brothers, Demetri and Nicco, teased
him mercilessly about his resemblance to their famous,
cousin—race-car driving sensation Emilio Morretti. And
although Rafael didn't see the physical similarities, he
suspected that's who the giggly blonde thought he was.
"I'm sorry, miss, but I think you have me confused with
someone else." He peeled her fingers off his forearm and
forced a smile. "I don't know you, and I'm certain you
don't know me."

She batted her fake eyelashes. "I know *exactly* who you
are and I can prove it."

"Okay," he said, deciding to call her bluff. "Who am I?"

"You're Rafael Morretti, heir to the Morretti Incorporated empire, and according to *Business Weekly,* one of the
most brilliant minds of the twenty-first century." Moving
closer, until they were touching, she lowered her voice to
a whisper. "You turned thirty-six back in August, but in
my opinion you don't look a day over twenty-five."

A grin found its way onto his lips. Rafael was impressed.
Not because the woman had memorized his personal bio,
but because she'd managed to recite his profile with a sin-
cere expression. As if she truly *was* his biggest fan.

"You were born in Italy, but presently reside in Washington D.C. You're single, you've never been married and you have no kids. Are you satisfied? Or should I go on?"

"No, I think you've said enough."

"Silly me. I forgot to introduce myself." She stuck out her chest and twirled a lock of hair around her index finger. "I'm Stefano's cousin, Julietta Via. You probably won't believe this, but I'm *very* well known in Italy."

Oh, I believe it! I bet you've tried to seduce every rich man in the country! As he stood there, listening to Stefano's cousin brag about her burgeoning modeling career, Rafael couldn't help wondering what he was doing wrong. Women like Julietta were always throwing themselves at him, sliding him their phone numbers and boldly propositioning him. These were the exact reasons he preferred to stay home on the weekends. He wasn't interested in finding Ms. Right, or making a love connection in Venice, either. He'd been disappointed by the opposite sex one too many times, and after his ex-girlfriend's bitter betrayal he'd decided to take a break from dating altogether. Rafael had no intention of getting played by another conniving woman desperate for fame and fortune. So he took a giant step away from the aggressive blonde and scanned the grounds for someone else to talk to.

"This is my favorite song," Julietta said, swaying to the sensuous beat of the music. "Let's get out there, and show everyone how to *really* get down."

Rafael shook his head. "I don't dance."

"Then let's take this intimate party for two inside the villa." She linked an arm through his and gestured to the French doors. "Follow me. I want to show you something."

"Are you always this forward?"

"I believe in taking life by the horns."

And I believe in staying far, far away from provocative women like you! Rafael spotted his brothers, slow dancing with their wives-to-be out on the floor, and felt a twinge of envy. These days, Demetri and Nicco were busy planning romantic dates and jetting off to the City of Lights, rather than hanging out with him. And for the first time ever Rafael was unfulfilled at work, and worried about his future. *Am I destined to spend the rest of my life alone?* he wondered, releasing a deep sigh. *Will I ever meet a woman who loves me for me, and not because of my net worth?* Ever since his younger brothers had gotten engaged, their mother, Vivica, had been on his case to settle down. And when she wasn't badgering him about finding a bride, she was trying to set him up on blind dates.

But Rafael had bigger problems than keeping his mother out of his personal life. Someone was out to ruin his family, and he had to find out who it was before it was too late. Terrifying things had happened over the summer, and even though his dad put up a brave front, Rafael could tell he was deeply concerned about Nicco's restaurant being vandalized, the shooting at the Beach Bentley Hotel and the recent arson attack. For that reason Rafael didn't bother to tell his father about the blackmail letters he'd received last Friday. He'd immediately turned the letters over to the police, though he knew there was little the cops could do. It was ultimately up to him and his security team to unearth the truth, and they would, no matter what.

"I want to get to know you better."

Rafael surfaced from his thoughts. "Is that right?"

"Absolutely," the blonde purred, brushing her lips against his cheek and a hand against his forearm once again. "Let's sneak inside for a quickie. No one will even notice we're gone."

Rafael had to admit it was a tempting offer, but he wouldn't do it. He wasn't looking for trouble, and Stefano's cousin could be the poster girl for Gold Diggers Anonymous. For all he knew, she was in cahoots with one of his business rivals, and he had no desire to end up on the cover of a sleazy Italian tabloid. Not when he was on the verge of finalizing a multimillion-dollar deal with one of the largest car manufacturers in the world. He had come to Venice for business, not pleasure, and it was imperative he keep his eyes on the prize, and off Julietta's jaw-dropping cleavage.

"I'm not interested."

"Of course you are," she argued, licking her lips lasciviously. "I can do things with my tongue that will make you scream…."

A rich, effervescent laugh filled the air, seizing Rafael's attention. It couldn't be, he told himself, shaking his head. No way she was there. Not in Venice, at his friend's wedding.

Another giggle reached his ears, louder and longer than the last. Rafael combed the tent, searching for the woman whose throaty, sultry laugh still gave him chills. His gaze landed on the bar, more than fifty feet away. And there *she* was. Paris St. Clair. How could he miss her? She'd been his first love, the only woman he'd ever felt an intense connection to, and even after all these years the sound of her voice still aroused him.

Her scarlet-red lips looked plump and juicy, her silky hair hung like a curtain over her shoulders, and she was dressed to kill in a black lace minidress. His eyes roved over her delectable shape. His pulse hammered in his ears, and his temperature shot through the roof. *Breathe, fool, breathe!*

Rafael stood at the back of the room, mesmerized, watching Paris dazzle her group of male admirers. Her radiant, butterscotch skin was glowing, her eyes shimmered under the decorative lights and her silky brown legs seemed to go on for miles. He was curious to know if she was married, how many children she had and if she'd fulfilled her dream of owning a beauty salon franchise.

But most important, he wondered if she'd ever thought of him over the years.

Rafael didn't realize he was moving until he heard the blonde's high-pitched voice fade into the background. With a dry mouth and a pounding heart, he strode purposely toward the bar. The beauty with the dazzling smile and bountiful curves sure looked like his ex, but Rafael had to know for sure if it was Paris, and there was only one way to find out.

Paris St. Clair loved having male attention. She stood at the bar discussing lucrative investment opportunities with a group of distinguished Italian businessmen worth millions. It was her job as maid of honor not only to tend to the bride, but to socialize with the other guests. Plus Paris knew if she continued flirting, and laughing at their jokes, they'd soon be putty in her hands.

Raising her champagne flute to her lips, she discreetly scoured the tent for anyone else wearing diamond watches and designer suits. No one caught her eye, but she made a mental note to introduce herself to the groom's family during dessert. Stefano Via came from old money, and although he never flaunted his wealth, Paris knew his father, a former mayor, was one of the richest men in the country. Definitely someone to get better acquainted with.

"So, what happened, little lady?" The media mogul with the salt-and-pepper hair grinned like the Cat in the Hat. "Did you hit the target or miss by a mile?"

Make them wait. It builds suspense! she thought, taking another sip of her champagne. Being a senior executive at her father's company, Excel Construction, had given her keen insight into the opposite sex. And holding center court among a group of rich, influential men was an exhilarating high. Being the "boss's kid" definitely had its downside, but Paris wouldn't trade working for her father, or her fabulous, jet-setting lifestyle, for anything in the world. She'd never forgotten her humble beginnings—all the times she'd gone to bed hungry as a child—and she was willing to do whatever it took to remain in the lap of luxury.

"I hit the bull's-eye on my first throw," she said proudly, shaking off the bitter memories of her past. "And when my brother fell into the dunk tank, he looked like he was going to cry!"

Tossing her head back, she laughed long and hard at the memory of Oliver shouting and flailing his arms in the dunk tank during Excel Construction's annual employee barbecue. Midgiggle, her gaze fell across a superfine man with light brown skin, a fitness trainer's build and the sexiest lips she had ever seen. The ground fell out from under her feet and her eyes widened in surprise.

Swallowing a gasp, she willed herself not to faint. Her heart was beating so loud and so fast she feared it would explode straight out of her chest. It was Rafael. Her first love. The guy she'd lost her virginity to; the man she'd once innocently believed was her soul mate.

Paris squinted, focused her gaze. Maybe her eyes were playing tricks on her. It wouldn't be the first time she'd mistaken a gorgeous Italian guy for her ex, and it probably wouldn't be the last. Their eyes met, zeroed in on each other, and Paris knew without a doubt it was Rafael. She'd recognize his smoldering stare and those long, thick eyelashes anywhere. Off-kilter, she gripped the side of the bar to keep from keeling over onto the manicured grass.

Eyes narrowed, she inspected him from head to toe. The years had obviously been kind to him. Back in the day, Rafael had been cute, but today he put the *h* in hot. His thick black hair was neatly trimmed, and he was immaculately groomed. His muscled physique filled out every inch of his tailored suit, and his boyish smile still made her heart swoon. He moved through the crowd with more confidence than one of Hollywood's leading men, and if that wasn't bad enough, charisma oozed from his pores.

Paris fanned a hand in front of her face, warning herself to get a grip. But he looked so dapper in his khaki suit that she couldn't help *but* stare at him. *This can't be real. I must be dreaming. What is Rafael Morretti doing here? And why is he headed my way?*

His cologne was a subtle fragrance, and as it wafted through the air her thoughts slipped back to the afternoon she'd lost her virginity to him at his family's beach house in Cape May. Did he remember that night? Paris quickly told herself it didn't matter. She didn't have time to relive the past, not when her past was staring her right in the face. Rafael was there, just inches away, and seeing him again gave her a heady feeling.

Desire rushed down her spine, tickling and teasing her most intimate parts. After all these years, she still wanted him, but Paris was determined not to embarrass herself.

To break the ice, she smiled. Rafael didn't.

"This is a pleasant surprise." His clipped tone suggested otherwise, but he had that twinkle in his eyes. A hungry, predatory expression on his face that said he was aroused. Back in the day, that look used to make her body tremble and quiver—

Still does, her conscience interrupted. *You're shaking so hard your teeth are chattering!*

"It's been, what, twenty years since we saw each other?"

No, fifteen years and three days, but who's counting? Feeling as if she was trapped in a mental fog, she gave her head a hard shake to clear her thoughts. Never in a million years did she expect to see Rafael at her best friend's engagement party. Questions raced through her mind. Did he still live in Washington? Did he have children? Was he married?

Of course he's married! her conscience shrieked. *Look at him! He's worth millions, he's built like a Greek god and his scent is as seductive as his smile.*

Years ago, he'd been featured in *Money* magazine, but the article didn't reveal any personal information about him. Currently, the rumor mill was filled with tales of embezzlement, lawsuits and infighting at Morretti Incorporated. But the most shocking story she'd heard recently was that Rafael's brothers, Demetri and Nicco, were happily in love. Deliriously in love, if the gossip blogs were true. The Morretti brothers used to be closer than the Three Musketeers, and Paris couldn't imagine any woman—no matter how beautiful she was—ever coming between them.

"It's wonderful to see you again." Commanding her legs to quit shaking, Paris leaned casually against the bar, as if she wasn't the least bit affected by his arrival. And she wasn't. She was a confident, thirty-five-year-old woman, not a shy, pubescent tween. She refused to let her nerves get the best of her. "It's been a long time, Rafael. How have you been?"

Rafael parted his lips, but his brain froze. Nothing came out. Not a word, not a squeak. Paris took his breath away— literally—and it demanded every ounce of his self-control not to sweep her up in his arms for a kiss. His tongue suddenly felt too big for his mouth, and it hurt to swallow. Struck dumb, he couldn't think of a single thing to say.

Rafael wanted to smack himself hard upside the head. *What's the matter with you, man? Why are you standing here gawking at her? She dumped you, remember?*

Standing tall, he masked his unease with a smile and slid his hands into the pockets of his dress pants. Damn, Paris made him feel nineteen again—like that quiet, socially awkward teenager who used to carry her books and walk her to class. *But I'm not a kid anymore,* he told himself, in an effort to bolster his confidence. *I'm an accom-*

plished businessman who out earns the president, so why the hell am I acting like a flustered, jittery fool?

"There you are. We've been looking all over for you."

Rafael turned, saw his brothers and shot them a puzzled look.

"Ms., do you mind if I steal my brother away for a few minutes?" Nicco asked.

"No, not at all. He's all yours." Paris placed her empty glass on the bar and tucked her purse under her arm. "It was great seeing you again, Rafael. Take care."

As she turned away, Rafael caught sight of the massive diamond ring on her left hand. Knowing that she belonged to another man should have tempered his desire, but it didn't. Paris was a stunner, hands down the most beautiful woman in the vicinity, and he hated to see her go.

"Damn, bro, are you okay?"

"Yeah, Demetri, I'm fine, but I wished you hadn't interrupted us."

Nicco wiped imaginary sweat off his forehead. "Thank God we did. You were drowning fast, bro. Five more minutes and you probably would have fainted at her feet!"

His brothers chuckled, but Rafael didn't appreciate their laughter at his expense. He wanted them to disappear, so he could track Paris down. She was married, and likely had children, but he'd rather spend time with her than with his wisecracking brothers. "All right, I admit it, seeing Paris again threw me off my game, but—"

"That was Paris St. Clair? The girl you were obsessed with in college?"

Rafael scowled. "Demetri, you're exaggerating. I wasn't obsessed with her."

"Yes, you were," Nicco argued, his tone matter-of-fact. "You wrote her love letters every day, and you slept with her picture under your pillow!"

"That was then, and this is now."

Demetri wore a skeptical look. "Are you sure? Because you were crushing on her pretty hard a few minutes ago."

"No, I wasn't. I was just making conversation."

Nicco chuckled long and hard. "You weren't. You were drooling like a Doberman with a raw steak bone!"

Chapter 2

"**W**hy didn't you tell me you invited Rafael Morretti to your wedding?" Paris burst into the master bedroom on the second floor of the twelve-room villa and cornered her best friend, Cassandra Knight, inside the enormous walk-in closet. "I almost fainted when I saw him!"

"What's the matter? Why are you so upset?"

Stumped, Paris closed her mouth. *What am I supposed to say? Seeing Rafael left me rattled. I'm still attracted to him. He's even more handsome at thirty-six than he was at nineteen....* Since she couldn't find the right words to express her feelings, she said nothing.

"You two should get along great. He's half Italian, and you love pasta, *and* Godfather movies. Sounds like a match made in heaven to me!"

"Knock it off," Paris snapped, annoyed by her friend's teasing. "This is serious."

Cassandra's face softened and she wore a sympathetic smile. "I know what this is about. You propositioned him and he shot you down, didn't he? I told you girl, less is more—"

"Rafael did not shoot me down."

Cassandra belted her robe and returned to the master bedroom. "Then why are you ranting and raving about a guy you just met?"

I know him better than you think, Paris thought, ambling over to the window. Pulling back the bronze drapes, she searched the grounds of the villa for her first love. Re-uniting with her old college sweetheart had stirred powerful feelings inside her, but even more shocking was the impulse she felt to jump his bones. *Maybe celibacy isn't such a good idea. I'm so horny I'm fantasizing about a guy I dumped fifteen years ago!*

"Keep your chin up. You'll meet a great guy this weekend. I just know it."

Paris scoffed and rolled her eyes to the vaulted ceiling. "Girl, please, I have a better chance of being struck by lightning during a snowstorm!"

"Okay, okay, fine, quit pouting. I'll get Rafael's phone number for you."

"I've known Rafael since I was a teenager," she blurted out, staring down at her bejeweled hands. The very same hands she'd once used to stroke Rafael's face, his chest and his… Paris deleted her last thought. To ward off the memories sneaking up on her, she pressed her eyes shut and took a deep, calming breath. "He was my first love."

"You hooked up with Rafael Morretti? No way!"

"We started dating our freshman year of college, and broke up a year later."

Cassandra wore a cheeky grin. "That means Rafael is Mr. O!"

"Don't call him that."

"What?" Her smile was coy, but the expression in her eyes was one of pure mischief. "You said your first love gave you orgasm after orgasm, night after glorious night."

"All right, all right," Paris snapped. "Enough already. I don't want to talk about my sexual escapades with Rafael Morretti."

"Don't get mad at me. They're your words, not mine."

Needing a distraction—something, anything, to take her mind off her old college sweetheart—Paris surveyed her surroundings. The seventeenth century villa was the perfect blend of Old World Venice and the modern, contemporary age. During the tour of the villa that afternoon, she'd learned it had a wine cellar, a personal theater and a home gym. But the room that impressed Paris the most was the study. Later, when the party died down, she was going to curl up on the couch and unwind with a romance novel.

"How was I supposed to know Stefano's childhood friend was your old college sweetheart?" Cassandra plopped down on the antique chair at the vanity table and unzipped her Hermes makeup bag. "I'm a savvy business-woman, Paris, *not* a mind reader!"

Paris laughed, but the uneasy feeling in her stomach remained. To take her mind off Rafael, she joined Cassandra at the vanity table and picked up a curling iron. "You're right. I'm sorry for blowing up at you, but seeing Rafael again after all these years has me on edge."

"Relax, you're getting yourself all worked up for nothing. Rafael is too much of a gentleman to rehash the past. Besides, he's leaving for Tuscany tomorrow, so you won't see him again until the wedding day."

"He balked at your ridiculous, five-page itinerary, too, huh? Smart man."

"I just want everyone I love to spend quality time together this week."

"I hear you, but a week-long wedding celebration is a little over the top, even for me."

"Don't talk to *me* about over the top. You rented out Spago for your thirtieth birthday, flew in friends from all across the country, and paid thousands of dollars to have Maxwell to perform," Cassandra said, nailing her with a don't-mess-with-me look. "Only celebrities do that, and the last time I checked your last name *wasn't* Kardashian!"

The friends laughed.

"Is, ah, Rafael, staying here, too?" Paris asked, keeping her tone light, casual.

"Of course."

"But I thought you rented the villa for the bridal party."

Cassandra frowned. "I did. Rafael is the master of ceremonies."

"Of what?"

"The wedding, Einstein!"

"And you're just telling me about this now!"

"Oh, I'm sorry," she said, eyebrows raised, her tone dripping with sarcasm. "I didn't realize I needed your approval before making decisions about *my* New Year's Eve wedding."

Paris ignored the dig. *Things just keep getting better!* Her gaze landed on the bedroom window overlooking the backyard. She recalled her conversation with Rafael, wondered why he had given her the cold shoulder. *Is he still mad about the way things ended?* Their exchange had been plagued with silence, and had felt like the longest minute of her life. Paris didn't want to stay at the villa, but she had few options. If she grabbed her stuff and left, Cassandra would flip out, and Paris didn't want to get on her girlfriend's bad side. "Are you sure Rafael's the right person to emcee the wedding? He's always been on the quiet side, and he hates public speaking."

"Don't be crazy. Of course I'm sure. He's incredibly charming," Cassandra said. "Once you get to know him you'll see what an amazing guy he is."

Girl, please, trust me, I know him. I've had that man in ways you wouldn't believe!

"Rafael only arrived a few hours ago, but the bridesmaids are already fighting over him. Even the ones with boyfriends!" she said with a laugh.

"They are? Really?"

"Yeah, Stefano's cousin, Julietta, told the other girls to back off or else."

Paris didn't like the sound of that. Not one bit. It was

insane that after all these years she was still attracted to
Rafael, but she was, and she didn't want him sowing his
wild oats while they were under the same roof. "Is there
anything else I should know?" she asked, twirling a lock
of Cassandra's hair around the base of the curling iron. "I
don't like surprises, and I have a feeling you're keeping
something from me."

"You're paranoid." With a grin, Cassandra added, "And
horny! You want Rafael so bad desire is practically oozing from your pores."

Paris wanted to tell her friend that she was dead wrong,
but couldn't get the words out. *Am I that transparent? Did
Rafael sense my desire? Is that why he ignored me earlier?*

"It's obvious you still like him, or you wouldn't be so
upset about seeing him again." Her tone was confident.
"Just admit it. You have the hots for him, and you want to
rekindle your romance."

"That's ludicrous. I haven't seen him in years."

"Yeah, but Rafael was your first boyfriend, your first
kiss, your first love—"

"I know, I know," Paris said glumly. "Don't remind me."

"As if you haven't relived that night a million times in
your mind." Cassandra sighed dreamily, as if her heart
was bursting with love, and touched a hand to her chest.
"You said your first time was the most magical moment
of your life."

"I was a teenager. It didn't mean anything."

"Good, so I don't have to worry about you and Julietta
fighting over him, right?"

"Don't worry. I'd never dream of doing anything to
ruin your big day."

Cassandra grabbed her hairbrush and pointed it at
the mirror. "You better not, or I'll kill you with my bare
hands!"

The women laughed. As Paris continued to style Cassandra's hair, they discussed the sightseeing excursion planned for tomorrow, and the wedding rehearsal at the world-famous Frari Church in the evening. Everything was in place for Stefano and Cassandra's New Year's Eve ceremony, and Paris was so excited for the couple that she was anxious for the big day to finally arrive. Just because she didn't believe in love, or the ridiculous notion of two people living happily ever after, didn't mean she couldn't support her best friend. Stefano was a great man, who treated Cassandra like a queen, and Paris was glad he'd finally popped the question and relocated to London to be with her. They were a dynamic couple, and Paris was thrilled that her friend was finally going to get her happy ending.

"If things get too overwhelming this weekend just let me know." A sad smile touched Cassandra's lips. "I'm here for you, Paris. Don't ever forget that."

"Quit stressing. I'm fine, really."

"I know, but I worry that all this wedding stuff is going to bring back painful memories."

Paris dropped her gaze to the floor and swallowed the lump in her throat. Sadness consumed her, caused her heart to pound erratically. Willing herself not to cry, she bit the inside of her cheek. Three years ago, she'd dated a man she'd hoped to build a life with despite her feelings for Rafael, and now she was alone, forced to deal with the pain of her ex-boyfriend's bitter betrayal.

Taking a deep breath, she cleared every troubling thought from her mind. Instead of dwelling on the past, she was going to focus on all the wonderful things in her life. She had a loving family, caring and supportive friends, and a successful career. Sure, she hated her job, and thought of quitting every day, but she'd rather suffer in silence than disappoint her father. Paris wanted to make him proud, craved and desired his approval more than anything in the world, and was determined to earn his respect.

"Have you spoken to Winston's mother recently?"

Paris nodded, but didn't elaborate on the hour-long conversation she'd had with the retired nurse days earlier. She couldn't talk about her ex-boyfriend's mother without getting emotional, and just thinking about the frail, elderly woman made her heart ache. She appreciated Cassandra's concern, but knew if she didn't change the subject *quick* she'd succumb to the clutches of grief and despair. And the last thing Paris wanted was to have an emotional breakdown.

"Don't move." Paris picked up the pink aerosol can on the vanity table, and sprayed Cassandra's elegant up-do with hair sheen. "Voilà, you're all done."

"I love it, girl, thanks!" Touching the nape of her neck, Cassandra turned from right to left, admiring her chic hairstyle. "When are you going to quit working for your old man, and finally open a high-end beauty salon?"

Paris groaned. "Not this again."

"Yes, *this* again. It's time you quit working for daddy dearest, and branch out."

"We've talked about this ad nauseam. I'm not cut out to run my own business."

"Of course you are," Cassandra argued, propping a hand on her hip. "You got your MBA from one of the finest business schools in the country, and you graduated at the top of our class."

Paris shook her head, refusing to give any thought to what her best friend said. Leaving Excel Construction wasn't an option. Even though she loved doing hair and makeup, and always dreamed of owning a salon, she wasn't about to leave her cushy executive job in Atlanta. Traveling the world, making great money and partying with wealthy, influential people was important to her. And if she quit working at her dad's company, she'd have to kiss her fabulous social life goodbye. "I opened a salon back in the day, and it was a complete failure, remember?"

"Don't be so cynical. You're older and wiser now. Things will be different."

"I can't afford to take that risk. I still owe my dad thousands of dollars. I'll be paying him back for many more years to come."

Cassandra stood, gripped Paris's shoulders and stared her down. "Then do what you do best—find some big-money investors and persuade them to back your salon."

Leaning against the vanity table, Paris gave some thought to what her friend had said. It was a good idea, but she didn't have the time or energy to take on such an enormous endeavor. Not when she had more responsibilities than ever. Besides, no one in their family ever defied her father, and Paris wasn't about to start.

"I'm going to go change." Selecting one of the dresses on the bed, Cassandra sashayed back inside the walk-in closet, and shut the door. Minutes later, she returned to the bedroom wearing a designer bejeweled gown. "How do I look?"

For effect, Paris hollered like a cheerleader. Her best friend had always been a low-key, no-fuss type of girl, but there she was, in her third dress of the night. She was draped in thousands of dollars' worth of diamonds, and her blue silk gown made her look as graceful as the Duchess of Cambridge. "I love the color of your dress, and how it shows off your killer bod. Your fiancé is one *very* lucky man!"

Giggling, the friends linked arms and exited the bedroom.

"We better hurry," Cassandra said, as they slowly descended the spiral staircase. "It's time for dessert, and if we're late there'll be nothing left. Julietta is a little, bitty thing, but boy, can that girl eat!"

Paris followed Cassandra through the grand foyer and out the French doors. Music, laughter and the pungent scents of fresh fruit and flowers filled the night air. With a dry mouth and an erratic heartbeat, Paris stepped inside the tent, hoping Rafael was long gone. At the thought of him, blood rushed through her veins. Try as she might, she couldn't squelch the butterflies swarming around her stomach. He had a hold on her still, after all these years. One Paris didn't understand, and couldn't explain. Memories sneaked up on her, scrolled through her mind in slow motion. The first time they'd kissed and the nights they'd made love were deeply cherished memories, ones she had relived hundreds of times over the years, and nothing would ever change how much she'd once loved and adored Rafael Morretti.

Once loved him? her conscience repeated. *When did you stop?*

To that, Paris didn't have an answer.

Chapter 3

Rafael sat in the media room, playing chess with Stefano, but he was having a hell of a time concentrating on the game. His thoughts were on Paris. Had been from the moment he'd laid eyes on her. Seeing his old college sweetheart again, after more than a decade, had his mind so twisted he couldn't think of anything *but* her. Stefano had won the last three games, and if that wasn't bad enough, he'd bragged about his landslide victories on Facebook and Twitter.

Realizing he didn't have a chance in hell of beating Stefano, Rafael threw his hands up in defeat and reclined in his leather chair. Low-hanging lights, plush furniture and colorful artwork gave the room a one-of-a-kind look. The air smelled of roasted peanuts, and the mouthwatering aroma made Rafael's stomach grumble. The wet bar was only a few feet away, but he was too tired to get up and fix himself a snack. It had been a day filled with surprises, and he still couldn't wrap his mind around Paris St. Clair being at his best friend's wedding celebration.

Raising his eyes to the ceiling, he contemplated calling it a night and heading upstairs to his bed. Paris was staying on the second floor, only three doors down from his room. And knowing that his ex—the woman he'd once loved more than anything in the world—was only a breath away would be the ultimate torture.

Rafael heard his cell phone chime, and glanced down at

the coffee table to read the number on the screen. His eyes narrowed, hardened with disgust. It was Cicely Cohen. His ex-girlfriend. The woman who'd betrayed his trust for fifteen minutes of fame. She'd been blowing up his phone for weeks, had left dozens of teary voice mail messages, but Rafael hadn't returned her calls. Wasn't going to, either. He had nothing to say to her, and the sooner she got the hint the better. They were over for good, and there was no way in hell he was taking her back.

"Rafael, is everything okay? You seem distracted."

"I'm cool, man. Don't worry about me," he said. "How are *you* feeling? The big day is fast approaching, so if you're having second thoughts, now's a good time to skip town!"

Stefano wore a proud smile. "Proposing to Cassandra last year in Aruba was the best decision I ever made, and I can't wait for her to become Mrs. Stefano Via."

"I'm glad to hear that. You're an incredible couple, and she definitely brings out the best in you." Rafael wanted to say more, but stopped himself in the nick of time. He couldn't fire off questions about Paris—not without raising suspicion—so for now he'd just have to cool his heels. "Have you guys decided where you're going to live after you get married?"

"We're going to stay in England for the time being. We love living in London and now that my consulting firm has taken off, I'm in no rush to return to the States."

"Congratulations, man. It sounds like everything has finally come together." Rafael picked up his wine cooler and took a swig.

"Where's Nicco?" Stefano asked. "I thought he was joining us for a nightcap."

"That's what he said, but Jariah probably had other ideas. My brother thinks he's running things, but make no mistake, his fiancée is the one in charge."

Stefano chuckled, and nodded in agreement. "I know what *that's* like, but I wouldn't have it any other way. If my woman's happy, then I'm happy. Cassandra means the world to me, and I'll never let anything come between us."

"You sound like an online dating ad!" Rafael joked.

"And you have no idea what you're missing. Now that I've found my soul mate I—"

"Have you met Paris's husband?" Rafael felt his cheeks burn, heard his pulse hammer in his ears, but faked a smile. It was too late to stuff the words back down his throat, and besides, he was curious to know about the man who'd captured his first love's heart.

"Who told you Paris was married?" Stefano asked, wearing a puzzled expression.

"She's not?"

His frown deepened, caused fine lines to wrinkle his forehead. "Nope, last time I checked she was single and ready to mingle!"

"But she's wearing a massive diamond ring on her left hand."

"Paris loves jewelry. Most women do."

Surprised, and oddly relieved by the news, Rafael pressed on. "Is she dating anyone?"

"Why? Are you interested?"

"I didn't come to Venice to make a love connection."

"Nicco said you dated Paris in college. How come you never mentioned her?"

He shrugged. "Because we weren't serious."

"Why did you guys call it quits?"

"What's with all the questions?"

"I just couldn't imagine you dating someone like Paris, that's all, and I wonder—"

"Someone like Paris?" he repeated, interrupting. "What's that supposed to mean?"

"You're polar opposites. She's a high-maintenance diva and you're Mr. Laid-back."

Rafael thought about what his friend had said, wondering if there was any truth to it. In college, Paris had been the girl every guy wanted, and every girl wanted to be. But he couldn't recall her ever copping an attitude with him, or behaving like a diva. Loved by everyone, and admired by all, she'd easily made friends. She had shone as the student council president, and gained the respect and admiration of the faculty and staff, as well.

Had Paris changed? Was she like all the other shallow, materialistic women he'd had the misfortune of dating in the past? Unlike his friends, Rafael didn't flaunt his wealth, and derived great pleasure from the simple things in life. Hot summer days spent jogging through the park with his beloved dogs; spending Sunday afternoons playing golf and watching football. He'd yet to find someone who loved the great outdoors, and humanitarian work, and doubted he ever would. Most women he met were more interested in driving around town in his Bentley and dining at five-star restaurants than getting to know him as person. And since he had more than enough work to keep him busy, he had zero interest in the Washington dating scene.

"Paris loves to party, and you're a recluse, so you'd definitely make an odd pair."

"Recluse? That's a stretch, don't you think?"

"No. The last time you went on a date Michael Jordan was still playing for the Bulls!"

Rafael had a zinger on his tongue, one he knew would wipe the grin clear off Stefano's face. But before he could speak, his friend resumed his interrogation.

"Did Paris cheat on you?" he asked in a solemn tone. "Is that why you broke up?"

"No, she transferred to Spelman her junior year, and the distance proved too much…." Rafael trailed off, stopping himself from saying more. What he didn't tell Stefano was that Paris had dumped him three days before his birthday and immediately started dating someone else. Some rich, good-looking clown on the football team. *It's in the past, water under the bridge,* he told himself, downing the rest of his wine cooler. *I moved on a long time ago, and never gave Paris, or her loser boyfriend, another thought.*

If that's true, his conscience said, *then why are you still bitter and resentful about your breakup? Why does your heart ache every time you see her?*

"I can't believe you're still sweet on her after all this time."

"Stefano, knock it off. I'm not sweet on Paris. I haven't seen her in years."

"So? Who's to say she's not the one?" he challenged, raising an eyebrow. He leaned forward expectantly. "Maybe it's true what they say. Maybe absence *does* make the heart grow fonder."

Rafael laughed, rejecting his friend's opinion with a dismissive flick of his hand. "Thanks for the advice, Dr. Love, but I'm not interested in making a connection with Paris or anyone else."

But I wouldn't mind a few nights of carnal pleasure, he thought as images of his ex-girlfriend bombarded his mind. Rafael couldn't remember the last time he'd had sex. Six months? A year? He told himself it didn't matter, because now that he'd reunited with his old college sweetheart his sexual drought was about to come to an abrupt end.

A grin tilted the corners of his lips. Seducing Paris was going to be more fun than playing high-stakes poker in Atlantic City. Rafael lived for the thrill of the chase, the pursuit, and he had a feeling the sexy socialite was going to make things very interesting this weekend. The only hurdle would be hooking up with Paris without everyone at the villa finding out. Rafael didn't want word of his holiday tryst getting back to his brothers, or worse, his matchmaking mother. He'd think of something, he had to, because tomorrow, when he saw Paris at breakfast, he was setting his plan in motion.

"I'm beat. I'm turning in." Stefano stood and swiped his iPhone off the coffee table. "Tomorrow's going to be a long day, and if I doze off during the tour Cassandra will kill me!"

"Is everyone heading into the city for the sightseeing excursion?"

"And by everyone, you mean Paris, right?" He wore a wry grin. "Yeah, she's going."

"I might tag along," Rafael said, keeping his tone light, casual. The thought of spending the day with Paris appealed to him, but he didn't confess the truth. If his best friend knew he was feeling something for her—even just a little—he'd blab to Cassandra, and Rafael didn't want anyone to know he was interested in hooking up with his former flame. "My meeting has been pushed back to Monday, and I have nothing planned tomorrow."

"That's great. Now you'll have time to romance Paris!"

Rafael scoffed at the suggestion. Ever since Stefano had proposed to Cassandra he seemed hell-bent on hooking him up with one of her single friends. And when he wasn't playing matchmaker he was bragging about his lady love. Stefano couldn't go five minutes without talking about how great she was, and listening to his buddy gush about his bride-to-be made Rafael feel lonelier than ever.

First my best friend finds love, and then my brothers, he thought, releasing a deep sigh. *Coming to Venice was a bad idea. All this love and happiness is sickening.*

"I'll meet you on the tennis court at 7:00 a.m.," Stefano said, as they exited the media room. "Don't be late, or I'll send Julietta to come get you."

"You better not, or you'll be sporting a black eye on your wedding day."

Chuckling good-naturedly they strode down the hall and climbed the staircase.

"Good night, man."

"Try not to snore," Rafael teased, clapping his friend on the back. "I'm a light sleeper, and I need my rest so I can whip you in straight sets tomorrow."

"Keep dreaming, pretty boy, it's not going to happen!"

Seconds later, Rafael opened his bedroom door, flipped on the lights and kicked off his shoes. The first thing he noticed was Julietta—sitting on the king-size bed in a flimsy lace negligee.

"I can't sleep," she stated. Her eyes were as wide and as innocent as Bambi's, but the mischievous expression on her tanned face told another story.

"What are you doing *here?*" Rafael retorted.

"I came to see you," she purred, flinging the blanket aside and hopping to her feet. Meeting his gaze head-on, she stalked toward him like a jaguar prowling the jungle for fresh meat. "Let's get down and dirty. I have wine, and more toys than a dominatrix!"

"I'm not interested."

"Then I'll just have to change your mind." Julietta reached for his belt buckle, but Rafael grabbed her hands. "What are you doing? Don't you want to have a good time?"

"It's late, and I have work to do."

"You don't want me to stay?"

"No, sorry, I don't."

Her smile fell away, and a sneer stained her glossy red lips. "I don't need this crap. I'm superpopular here, and there are plenty of guys who'd kill to be with me," she argued, propping her hands on her wide, full hips. "I was the third runner up in last year's Miss Italia contest, and I have more Twitter followers than the Dalai Lama...."

To end her rant, Rafael opened the bedroom door. "Good night, Julietta. Sleep well."

"If you change your mind, which I *know* you will, I'll be skinny-dipping in the pool."

Rafael watched the blue-eyed temptress slink down the staircase, convinced that things couldn't get any worse. But as he turned away, he spotted Paris standing at the other end of the hall, staring at him. He wanted to tell her about what *didn't* happen with Julietta, but he could tell by the malevolent glare on Paris's face that she thought he was the scum of the earth. But he had to say something, had to defend himself. Before Rafael could utter a word she marched into her bedroom and slammed the door.

Chapter 4

On Friday morning downtown Venice was clogged with noisy tourists, and flamboyant street performers hoping to make a quick buck, but Rafael couldn't keep his eyes off Paris. Standing in the middle of the world-famous Piazza San Marco was a mind-blowing experience, one that should have been captivating enough to hold his attention, but it didn't. Not with Paris around.

She looks like an angel, Rafael thought, admiring her on the sly. Her oversize sunglasses gave her a youthful air, her crimson lips held a dazzling smile and her sleeveless white dress played up her pear-shaped figure.

Yeah, a naughty angel you'd love to see naked, his conscience taunted. *Quit gawking at her. You're better than that. You're a Morretti, remember?*

But Rafael didn't turn away. He lacked the willpower and fortitude it required. Paris was dressed to kill, and her traffic-stopping curves made him hot under the collar *and* below the belt. Diamonds dangled from her ears, neck and wrists, and her ankle bracelet drew his gaze down her long legs time and time again.

"The Piazza San Marcos is one of the most beautiful places in Italy, and people travel from far and wide to admire the magnificent works of Antonio Canova, Giovanni Bellini and Vittore Carpaccio."

Rafael tore his gaze away from Paris, and turned his attention to the middle-aged tour guide with the receding

hairline. He tried to listen to what Mr. Esposito was saying, but all he could think about was kissing Paris with all
the passion coursing through his veins. He wouldn't act
on his feelings, knew better than to make a move on her
in public, but dammit if he didn't want to.

That morning at breakfast he'd scored a seat beside
her. But unfortunately Paris had spent more time chatting
with the other groomsmen than talking to him. And when
they did speak their conversation was plagued with tension
and awkward silences. No matter, Rafael told himself. He
wasn't giving up. They'd had something special once, and
he liked the idea of having a holiday fling with Paris in
his beloved hometown. In fact, he couldn't think of a better way to kick off the New Year. He was determined to
connect with his old college sweetheart and nothing was
going to stop him.

Raising his water bottle to his lips, he took a long, refreshing drink. The sky was clear, the breeze thick and
the air was filled with the scent of sweet-smelling flowers.
People were everywhere—snapping pictures, feeding the
pigeons, wandering the cobblestone streets and pushing
and shoving like kids waiting in line at the water fountain.
As Rafael moped the sweat from his brow he decided he'd
had enough excitement for one day.

He choked down more water. After hours of walking
from one ancient monument to the next, he was ready to
head back to the villa for some R & R. He'd been up since
dawn, and after working on his presentation, he'd played
tennis with Stefano and swam in the heated pool.

Checking his gold wristwatch, Rafael was surprised to
see that it was midday. After lunch, the group was heading
over to the fashion district. He had no desire to go shopping, and had better things to do with his time, but knew
it was a bad idea to ditch the group. If he did, one of the
other groomsmen would make a move on Paris, and there

was no way in hell Rafael was letting that happen. He'd have to suck it up, and bide his time.

"Are we going on a gondola ride today?" asked one of Stefano's short, plump aunts.

The tour guide wore a polite smile. "No, ma'am, I'm afraid not."

"But it's on the top of my bucket list, and I may never come to Italy again!"

Everyone in the group laughed. The bride and groom's friends and family—sixty-five loud, boisterous people in all—entered the Campanile, the city's oldest and tallest building. But Rafael noticed Paris ducking into one of the nearby bakeries.

Curious, he entered the *pasticceria* and took off his Ray-Ban sunglasses. A fruity, spicy aroma sweetened the air, stirring his senses and rousing his appetite. With its sultry lights, timber chandeliers and glass sculptures, the shop looked more like an art gallery than a pastry store. Italian music was playing, and the servers looked as chic as the decor.

Rafael looked around, but couldn't find Paris anywhere. As he sat down on one of the raised, wooden stools, he spotted a buxom waitress climbing the circular, white staircase. Rafael contemplated heading upstairs to scope out the second floor, but decided against it. Trailing Paris was a bad idea. They had plenty of time to get reacquainted, and since he didn't want her to think he was stalking her, he'd hang out on the main floor, have a cup of coffee and watch the world go by from his window seat.

His cell phone chirped, alerting Rafael that he had a new text message. He took his iPhone out of his backpack and punched in his password. Reading the message from Gerald Stanley gave him a surge of adrenaline. His security advisor was one step closer to single-handedly cracking the case.

I just got off the phone with my source at Miami PD. Gracie O'Conner has no alibi for the night of the arson, and neither does her ex-con brother.

Rafael was pleased with the work Gerald had done, and sent a short, quick response.

The suspects in the case were obvious, so why hadn't the police made any arrests? he wondered. Why were they taking their sweet-ass time bringing the perpetrators to justice? Gracie O'Conner, Nicco's former assistant, was a scheming manipulator with an ax to grind. And although she was a petite, soft-spoken woman, Rafael's gut feeling was that she was involved in the crime. But Gracie wasn't the only one who hated his family. His father had made a lot of enemies over the years, and Rafael wouldn't be surprised if one of his dad's old business rivals was out to destroy him.

His cell phone rang, and the sound yanked Rafael out of his troubled thoughts. He didn't recognize the number, but saw the area code, and knew the person was calling from Washington, D.C. "This is Rafael Morretti."

"Hello, Mr. Morretti," said a husky female voice. "My name is Danica Lyons."

The name didn't ring a bell, so he waited for the woman to explain who she was. It was 5:00 a.m. on the East Coast, and Rafael couldn't image why someone he didn't know would be calling him first thing in the morning. After a moment of silence, he asked the question at the front of his mind. "How did you get my phone number?"

"It doesn't matter. I'd like to speak to you privately, and the sooner the better."

Rafael frowned. He turned her words over in his head, but they still didn't make any sense. "I'm sorry, Ms. Lyons, but I'm afraid I don't understand what this is pertaining to."

"I'd rather not discuss the matter on the phone," she said

in a crisp tone. "I'd like to come to your office tomorrow to speak in person."

"I'm out of the country, and won't be back in Washington until January 3."

"Don't play games with me, Mr. Morretti, or things will get real ugly for you."

Taken aback by her abrupt rudeness, Rafael stared down at the phone, unable to believe what he was hearing. "Are you threatening me?" he asked, struggling to control his temper. "Because if you are, this conversation is over."

"I'm not threatening you, Mr. Morretti. I'm simply stating a fact."

Rafael struggled to not lose his cool. Keeping his head was paramount, so he took a deep breath and cleared his voice of emotion. "Call my office, and my secretary will book you an appointment."

"Very well. I look forward to meeting you."

What the hell? Rafael hit the end button and immediately dialed Gerald's number to tell him about his bizarre conversation with Danica Lyons. He suspected she knew something about the arson investigation, so he asked Gerald to do a background check on her. Everyone everywhere wanted to get their hands on the Crime Stoppers reward, and although Rafael didn't put much faith in the Washington PD solving the case, he refused to leave any stone unturned.

Seconds later, when he'd ended his phone call with Gerald, Rafael felt as if a weight had been lifted from his shoulders. He had nothing to worry about. By the end of the week he'd have a detailed, comprehensive report on Danica Lyons, and he was looking forward to reading every salacious word.

He slung his backpack over his shoulder and slowly perused the circular glass cases in the upscale pastry shop. After ordering a latté, he bought gourmet chocolates for his mom, Italian cookies for his father and amaretto brownies for his brothers, and paid to have them delivered to the villa.

At the cash register, Rafael spotted Paris. She was standing in front of the elaborate cake display, snapping pictures of it with her cell phone. Tapping her foot, she swayed to the beat of the music, rocking her hips provocatively from side to side. Her moves were hypnotic, and like a drunk guzzling Cristal, he was hooked. She was close enough to touch and caress, but instead of reaching out to stroke her sinuous curves, he looked away, stuffing his hands deep into the pocket of his blue jeans.

He picked up on the whispered conversation of two dark-haired men nearby as they pointed at Paris, obviously admiring her beauty. His chest automatically puffed up with pride. An odd response, considering she wasn't his girlfriend, but Rafael couldn't help the way he felt. Nothing had changed. If anything, Paris was more captivating and appealing. She was as vivacious as ever, and everywhere she went people gravitated to her. As he continued to watch her sway and groove to the music, he could see why.

Rafael glowered menacingly at the cocksure businessmen, who were speaking in rapid-fire Italian. His hands balled into tight fists and his heartbeat thundered inside the walls of his chest. The men were discussing how to lure Paris into bed, and even joked about filming the encounter and posting it online. Their conversation was none of his business, but Rafael felt compelled to say something. Had to before he lost his temper and pummeled them both into the ground.

Rafael spoke to the men in an authoritative voice, and scowled for good measure

Back off, fellas. The lady's with me? his conscience repeated. *How original!*

"W-we're sorry," stammered the man with the mustache. "We didn't mean any disrespect. We were just joking around."

The two took off through the side door, and Rafael sighed in relief. Crisis averted. Nothing wrong with telling a little white lie, he decided, tasting his coffee. It was either that or lose Paris to someone else, and he wasn't about to let that happen. Rafael didn't want anyone to ruin his chances with her—

Your chances of what? his conscience questioned.

Paris must have sensed him behind her, because she glanced over her shoulder, then hit him with a pointed look. But when she spoke her tone was rife with amusement. "See anything you like?"

Do. I. Ever! His mouth watered and his temperature soared. The view of her big, beautiful backside made an erection swell inside his jeans. Her eyes lit up like stars when she laughed, and she smelled sweeter than the desserts inside the pastry shop. "The truffles look good," he said casually, gesturing at the wall behind her. "I think I might get a few packages for my soon-to-be-sister-in-law. Angela loves chocolate almost as much as she loves Demetri!"

"So, the rumors *are* true." Paris dropped her cell phone inside her purse and gave him her undivided attention. "Your brothers found love, and are both getting married next year. How exciting! Is it a double wedding? When are they tying the knot? Where is the venue?"

His jaw stiffened like clay, but he managed a weak smile. He didn't want to talk about his brothers or their future wives. Not here, not now. But if he changed the subject Paris would think he was rude. Or worse, jealous, and he wasn't.

Rafael averted his gaze and raked a hand over his hair. He tried not to think about how lonely he was, how empty he felt inside. These days he hardly saw his brothers, and when he did they droned on and on about their fiancées. Especially Nicco. He was the worst perpetrator. He adored Jariah and her six-year-old daughter, Ava, and over the past three months the trio had developed a strong bond, one he talked about nonstop. At times it was funny, endearing even, but at other times it got on Rafael's nerves.

He was happy his brothers had found their soul mates, but he didn't want to discuss their love lives. He was dying to know more about Paris—where she lived, what she did for work, if she was dating anyone—and he didn't want to waste time chatting about wedding nonsense. "I'm the wrong person to ask. I don't even remember when the wedding is, and I'm the best man!" he joked good-naturedly.

"Are you sure Nicco's ready to get married?"

Her question surprised him, gave him pause. "Yeah, why?"

"Because I was at the grand opening of Dolce Vita Atlanta and he was flirting with everybody!"

Rafael chuckled. "He wasn't engaged back then. Jariah started working for Morretti Incorporated last summer, and apparently they hit it off immediately. Nicco says it was love at first sight, but the jury is still out on that one!"

"So do you like her?"

"Yes, of course." He thought back to the first time he'd met Jariah, and cringed inwardly when he remembered the unflattering things he'd said about her to Nicco. His brother had always had horrible taste in women, and he'd feared that Jariah was another gold digger. Thankfully, she wasn't, and the more time Rafael spent with the hardworking single mother, the more he admired her. "Any more questions, Katie Couric?"

"Excuse me for trying to make conversation," she said with a laugh. "I was surprised to see you get on the tour bus this morning. Aren't you supposed to be doing business in Tuscany?"

Rafael wore a puppy dog face. "You're keeping tabs on me. I'm touched."

More laughter passed between them.

"My meeting was pushed back to Monday, so I decided to join the group," he explained, admiring her radiant brown skin. "Why are you hiding out in here? You're supposed to be at the bell tower with everyone else."

Paris picked up her wicker basket, slipped her hand inside a white package and tossed a chocolate-covered cashew into her mouth. "I got hungry."

"You always did like your sweets."

"Still do," she quipped. "Cassandra forced me to go on the soup diet with her, and if she finds out I cheated she'll go ballistic, so don't tell her you saw me in here, okay?"

"I won't tell a soul. Your secret is safe with me."

Paris walked over to the cash register, unloaded her items on the marble counter and paid the cashier. Seconds later, she joined him at the entrance of the store. "What's your story?" she asked, slipping on her oversize Givenchy sunglasses. "Why did you ditch the group?"

Because I want to be alone with you, he thought, but didn't say. It was too much too soon, and he didn't want to scare her off. Not when they were enjoying each other's company. To keep the mood light, he said, "I got tired of Cassandra's foster mom hitting on me, so I decided to make a break for it when she wasn't looking!"

Paris cracked up. The sound of her high-pitched giggles bolstered his confidence. He couldn't have scripted a better reunion.

"It was great talking to you, Rafael. See you around!" she said suddenly, walking closer to the door.

He caught her arm just as she was about to breeze past him, and slid in front of the door to prevent her from leaving. "Where are you rushing off to?"

A frown touched her lips, marring her pretty features,

but she didn't speak. His body was a raging inferno and his impulse to kiss her was so strong it consumed him. He wet his lips with his tongue, moved closer. "Don't go." His voice sounded foreign to his ears, a lot huskier than it had ever been. "I'll escort you to the bell tower."

"I'm not going there. The group is slowing me down, and I have tons of shopping to do."

An idea came to him, and a lie fell smoothly from his lips. "You have to shop and I have to shop, so we might as well knock it out together."

"Are you sure your paramour won't mind? I don't want to create any problems at home."

I'm not interested in Julietta. I'm interested in you.

"You guys looked awfully cozy last night," Paris continued. "And she's also made it very clear to the bridal party that you're off-limits."

"Paris, I'm single, and there's no special woman in my life, but if you feel uncomfortable hanging out with me, then…"

Her frown deepened. "Why would I be uncomfortable?"

"Because we had a messy breakup."

"Yeah, like twenty years ago," she scoffed, giving him a funny look. "We dated when we were kids. It didn't mean anything. I moved on and so did you. No hard feelings."

Listening to Paris downplay their relationship hurt like hell, but Rafael held his tongue. Besides, she was right. They'd dated eons ago, and living in the past was a waste of time. "So, you don't mind if I tag along? I promised my dad I'd buy him a case of Italian cigars, and if I forget he'll cut me out of his will!"

Paris wore a cheeky smile. "Sure, why not? You could help me carry my bags."

"First we eat and then we shop."

"When did you get so bossy?" she teased, slanting her

head to the right. "What happened to the sweet, easygoing guy who used to let me call the shots?"

Rafael lowered his mouth to her ear. "He grew up."

"I can see that."

"And what you call bossy, I call decisive," he said smoothly. "I don't believe in playing games. When I see something I want, I go after it. No matter what."

Her eyes opened wide.

The air was saturated with the scent of his desire. Rafael wanted to crush his lips to her mouth, wished he could taste her one more time, but he didn't act on his impulses. To keep his hands busy, and off her curvy, shapely body, he stepped aside and opened the door. "Shall we go? I'm hungry, and I bet you are, too."

"Where are we going?"

"To the best Italian restaurant in town, of course."

Her face came alive, brightened with excitement. "Now you're talking. Lead the way!"

Chapter 5

Harry's Bar, a ridiculously expensive pub in the heart of the city, was more than just a classy restaurant, it was a cultural institution. Open since the 1930s, it attracted Venetian high society, diplomats and celebrities from around the globe. The menu was simple, and the furnishings understated, but the award-winning food more than made up for the modest decor.

"Might I recommend the Cipriani chocolate cake for dessert?" The waiter, an older gentleman with kind eyes, collected Paris and Rafael's empty lunch plates and refilled their water glasses. "It's our most celebrated dish, and one of the First Lady's personal favorites."

"Sounds good," Rafael said. "We'd also like another round of Bellini cocktails."

The waiter gave a curt nod. "Very well, sir. I'll be back shortly with your order."

"You have to quit feeding me, or I won't be able to fit into my gown tomorrow!" Paris joked, settling back comfortably in her chair. "I don't want to get on the bride's bad side—"

"Don't worry, Paris. I'll be there to protect you."

He flashed a grin, and her breath caught on a moan. The second floor was filled to the brim with distinguished diners, and waiters in shiny bow ties rushing to and fro, but when Rafael looked at her everyone else faded into the background.

His gaze roamed over her face, warmed her tingling flesh. Desire blazed in his eyes, and for a pulse-pounding second Paris feared he was going to kiss her. *What should I do if he does? Push him away, kiss him back or make a break for the emergency exit?*

Swallowing hard, she moistened her lips with her tongue. Her attraction to Rafael was ruling her, mind and body, and if she didn't get a handle on her feelings quick she was going to fall victim to her desires. *And there's nothing cute about pouncing on a man in public.*

"The Cipriani chocolate cake is the pièce de résistance, and I can't let you leave Venice without trying it. Trust me, you're going to love it."

"God, you're smooth," she quipped. "Now I know why Julietta's been throwing herself at you all weekend. You're as charming as they get!"

"She's not interested in me per se, just my bank account."

"That's a harsh assessment. You hardly know her."

"I know her type." A frown wrinkled his brow, caused fine lines to gather around his eyes and mouth. "Tell me something."

"Ask away. What's on your mind?"

Rafael picked up her left hand, gently caressed each finger. Electricity crackled between them, and the more he stroked her skin the harder it was for Paris to concentrate.

"You're single, right?"

All she could do was nod her head. Her mind was too jumbled to produce a coherent thought. She tried to ignore the flutter in the pit of her stomach, that tingling sensation shooting down her spine, but to no avail. *He's just a man,* scolded her conscience. *Sure, he's tall, ripped and toned, but that's no reason to get nervous and flustered.*

His caress was better than she remembered. Paris told herself to breathe, to stare at something—anything—

besides Rafael's lips, but she couldn't tear her gaze away from his face. Her desire for him was strong, so intense it made it impossible for her to think. Moving her hand away was out of the question too. Paris loved how he'd always made her feel desirable, wanted and sexy. "I date from time to time," she said, twirling a lock of hair around the index finger of her free hand. "But I'm single, and have no plans to settle down."

"Then why are you wearing an expensive diamond ring?"

To keep the opposite sex at bay. Talking about her ex-boyfriend always made her tear up, and since she didn't want to have an emotional breakdown at their quaint corner table, Paris racked her brain for a suitable answer. Wanting to keep the mood upbeat, she said, "I love diamonds. Sue me!"

"I understand that, but why not wear the ring on your other hand?"

His question caught her off guard. No one had ever grilled her about her diamond ring before, but then again, she'd never let anyone get this close. Men were good for one thing and one thing only. After the deed was done Paris went home—alone. Pillow talk wasn't an option, and neither was spending the night with her lover. "You're a guy. You wouldn't understand."

Rafael released her hand and sat up straighter. "Try me."

"I'm good at my job and I take great pride in what I do, but my clients are more interested in flirting with me than listening to what I have to say."

"Do you blame them?" His tone changed, becoming playful, and amusement twinkled in his deep brown eyes. "You're stunning, you have a wicked sense of humor, and sensuality and femininity literally ooze from your pores. They can't help themselves!"

His words made her heart melt, but Paris didn't let her

feelings show. No use encouraging him. Their lunch date was a onetime thing, and despite their attraction, Paris had no desire to strike up any kind of relationship with her ex. She didn't do long-distance, and hated the thought of being tied down to one person.

"Aren't you afraid of scaring off Mr. Right?"

Paris laughed, and shrugged off his question with a flick of her hand. "I'm too busy being successful to worry about being single. Besides, Mr. Right doesn't exist, and neither does the ridiculous notion of living happily ever after."

"You sound like a pessimist."

"I'm not a pessimist. I'm a realist. Instead of wasting my time dating, I'm focusing my energy on climbing the corporate ladder, and expanding my father's lucrative business empire."

"Don't you get lonely?"

"Do you?" she asked, flipping the tables. "You're thirty-six. Isn't it time you quit sowing your wild oats and find a nice Italian girl to marry?"

"Have you been talking to my mother?"

His laughter filled the dining room, and the sound made her giggle. Joking around with Rafael made Paris feel good, better than she had in weeks. He was an honest-to-goodness gentleman, who said and did all the right things, and who knew how to make a woman feel special. Paris liked that. He was unique, interesting, nothing like the men most of her girlfriends complained about, and she was having a great time with him. "Have you ever been married?" she asked, her curiosity getting the best of her. "Do you have children?"

"No, and I'm in no rush to have a family." A wicked grin curved his mouth. "I'll settle down as soon as I meet a smart, vivacious beauty like you, and not a minute sooner."

"Then you're going to be single for a *very* long time, because I'm one in a million!"

"That's what I thought the first time I ever laid eyes on you." He sounded serious, as if he meant every word, and his gaze smoldered with intensity. "You looked so cute in your sundress and cowboy boots I just knew I had to meet you. You were the prettiest girl in the room. Still are."

His confession blew her mind. "I can't believe you remember what I wore to the spring formal our freshman year at Georgetown."

"How could I forget? It was a special day."

That it was, she thought, her cheeks flushed with heat. *We did a whole lot of French-kissing and slow dancing that night, and by the time you walked me back to my car I was in love!*

"I remember a lot of things about you—"

"Really? Like what?" Paris didn't believe him, not for a second, so she put him on the spot. "What's my favorite color?"

"That's easy, purple."

Without a doubt, his megawatt smile was his best feature, and Paris could tell that he was proud of himself for answering the question correctly. Their banter was effortless, easily the highlight of her day. "Is that all you've got?"

He stroked his jaw as if deep in thought. "You used to love horror movies, the Backstreet Boys and chocolate fudge milkshakes from Dairy Queen."

"I still do!" she shrieked, laughing. "How do you think I got so curvy?"

"Paris, you're stunning and you know it."

"And you're too charming for your own good!"

The waiter arrived with their order and conversation was put on hold. Paris took a bite of her cake, enjoying the strong, rich flavor. As they ate, they discussed Stefano and Cassandra's New Year's Eve wedding, their families and their careers.

"I'm surprised that you work for your father's construction company."

Paris felt her eyebrows rise, and her shoulders tense. She was used to people taking cheap shots at her, knew what her colleagues said behind her back, and normally she didn't care. But what Rafael said ticked her off. "Why are you surprised? You don't think I'm smart enough to work in a male-dominated industry?"

"I'm not even going to dignify that question with a response."

His voice was cold, and his gaze was deadly. He was annoyed with her, but for some odd reason that turned her on, made her wonder if he was still a passionate lover.

"Your dream was to start a beauty salon franchise, and I figured by now you'd have dozens of high-end shops around the world."

Paris picked up her water glass. "Dreams change."

"Do you enjoy being a senior administrator at your father's company?"

No, she thought sadly, *but I have no choice. I'm stuck. My father will never let me leave the family business, and furthermore, I'm a St. Clair. According to my dad, St. Clairs don't give beauty treatments, they get beauty treatments.*

"Yes, of course," she lied, avoiding his probing gaze. "I'm very good at my job, and I'm proud of what Excel Construction has accomplished over the years. We've constructed schools, health clinics and community centers in inner city neighborhoods, and we have even more incredible projects lined up in the New Year."

"Any chance of you opening a salon one day?"

"Been there, done that, and I'm not going there again."

"It sounds like your past venture failed to meet your expectations."

"That's the understatement of the year," she murmured.

Rafael leaned forward in his chair. "What happened?"

"Trust me, it's a long, boring story. You wouldn't be interested."

Without a moment's hesitation, he said, "I wouldn't have asked if I didn't want to know. Go on."

Paris parted her lips, and to her surprise the truth came tumbling out. "I opened a salon with one of my sorority sisters from Spelman after graduation, and it turned out to be the biggest mistake of my life. If not for my father stepping in, and cleaning up the mess I made, I'd still be in court duking it out with my ex-best friend."

"Paris, you can't let one bad experience stop you from fulfilling your dreams."

"That's easy for you to say," she argued. "Everything you touch turns to gold!"

"It wasn't always that way," he confessed, his tone subdued. "I screwed up a lot my first few years at Morretti Incorporated, but after each failure, I picked myself up, dusted myself off and vowed to learn from my mistakes."

Shocked, Paris closed her open mouth. "You struggled to find your footing in the business world, too?"

"Absolutely, and I'm a better man because of all the hardships I faced. It forced me to challenge myself, and to think outside of the box."

He spoke with such fire and intensity that her thoughts took an erotic detour. Paris loved how strong he was, how intelligent, and his confidence was damn sexy.

Rafael picked up his water glass and took a drink. "The only way you lose in life is if you beat yourself, and I'm determined to be at the top of my game no matter the cost."

Damn, Paris thought, licking her lips. *I wish you were on top of* me.

"You're very passionate about what you do," she said. "I admire that."

"I think my ambition and my intensity has been the

key to my success. Being the vice chairman of Morretti
Incorporated is more than just a career. It's my life, and I
feel fortunate to be doing something I love. A lot of people aren't that lucky."

Tell me about it. Releasing a deep sigh, Paris toyed
with her chain-link necklace. Owning a high-end salon—a
trendy, glamorous place where women went to network, socialize and relax—would be a dream come true. But Paris
was scared of falling flat on her face. It had already happened once, and it could again. "I love the idea of going
into business for myself, but my father would never give
me his support."

"Why do you need his approval?"

Good question. Why indeed?

"You're a smart, intelligent woman who can do anything she sets her mind to."

I am! Paris considered what Rafael had said, and realized he was dead-on. *My dad didn't consult me when he
married his trophy wife from hell, so why should I consult
him about going into business for myself?*

"Why are you looking at me like that?" she asked, picking up her napkin and dabbing the corners of her mouth.
"Do I have chocolate icing on my face or something?"

"No, you look perfect." He shrugged and said, "I was
just wondering what our lives would have been like if we
didn't split up."

"Sure you were," she quipped, her tone filled with sarcasm. "Just admit it. You haven't thought about me since
our breakup, and the only reason you recognized me last
night was because you overheard someone at the party
say my last name."

Rafael didn't miss a beat. "I knew it was you the moment I heard your laugh."

"No way. Seriously?"

"Once you love someone, they always stay in your heart.

Contrary to what you think, I never forgot about you. You were my first love, and I wanted to marry you."

"Rafael, we were kids."

"No, we weren't. Quit saying that."

His sharp tone and the strength of his gaze shocked her.

"We were nineteen, and we both knew exactly what we were doing." Rafael cracked a smile. "And if my memory serves me correctly you kissed me first."

I sure did, and I loved every minute of it! Paris swallowed a moan, and buried her hands in her lap. Talking about the past would inevitably lead to daydreaming about all the times they'd laughed, and kissed. If she wanted to keep her wits about her she had to guard her mind against her memories.

She picked up her handbag and checked the time on her cell phone. Enough flirting with Rafael. Lunch was over, and not a moment too soon. "Thanks for lunch. This was nice."

"You're most welcome. It was my pleasure." Rafael strode around the table and pulled out her chair. "After you."

Standing, she took the hand he offered and slipped on her sunglasses. Paris was wearing her favorite pair of high-heeled shoes, but Rafael still towered over her. He was six feet six inches of drop-dead sexy, and being in the presence of such a gorgeous, virile man was doing one hell of number on her libido. Making love to Rafael was inconceivable, but when he rested a hand on the small of her back, it was all Paris could think of. He was her first love, and he'd always have a special place in her heart, but that was the extent of it. Paris wasn't interested in rekindling their relationship, and as long as she remembered that all men were dogs—even charming, well-bred guys like Rafael—she'd never have to worry about being betrayed by a lover again.

Chapter 6

Rafael spent the rest of the afternoon strolling around the crowded, bustling streets of Venice with Paris. They admired the extravagant window displays, the gothic architecture of ancient buildings, and relished being in one of the most breathtaking cities in the world. In the fashion district, they bought gifts for their families, tried on Venetian face masks and enjoyed a snack at a sidewalk cafe. As they drank wine and ate calzones, they laughed about their college days and watched the tuxedoed band perform at the city square.

"I don't know what to get." Paris stood at the front of the souvenir shop, holding a hanger in each hand, wearing a frown. "Which one do you like better? The T-shirt with the pasta shells or the boxer shorts covered with wine bottles?"

"They're both hideous, but if I had to pick one I'd choose the boxers."

Flashing a coy smile, she slanted her head to one side. "Are you sure you don't want a couple pairs? I think they're très chic, and totally you!"

Rafael chuckled. "I'm positive, but if I change my mind I'll let you know."

Foreign languages and boisterous laughter filled the air. The souvenir shop was just steps away from the Grand Canal and crammed with everything from postcards to shoes and housewares. Being in such a small, confined space, with dozens of other people, made Rafael uneasy but he was having a hell of a good time. Paris freely spoke her mind, no matter the topic, and he enjoyed hearing her colorful stories about her employees, her friends and her family.

"This shop has the coolest stuff." She picked up a cross-shaped rosary box and examined it. "My brother gave me a gag gift for Christmas, and now it's payback. I can't wait to see the look on his face when he opens the gondola condom holder!"

"How are your brother and sister doing?" Rafael leaned against the counter and slid his hands into the front pocket of his jeans. "Your niece is fifteen-years-old now, right?"

"Wow, you have an amazing memory," Paris said, her tone one of awe. "Bella's a high school junior, and she's already taller than me!"

"I bet she's just as beautiful as her aunt."

Paris winked, and patted his cheek. "Keep the compliments coming, and I'll buy you your *own* gondola condom holder!"

Rafael tossed his head back, and laughed long and hard. Her spirited, fun-loving nature appealed to the kid in him, and he loved her witty sense of humor.

"Kennedy is happily married with four children, but my brother, Oliver, is still as juvenile as ever. He'll be forty next year, but I'm starting to think he'll never grow up."

"Does Oliver work for your father, as well?"

"On paper, yes, but he rarely goes into the office. He'd rather play golf with his buddies than attend executive meetings."

"Be patient. Your brother will find his way."

"I hope so, because I'm sick of doing his job *and* mine!"

At the cash register, as Paris loaded her items onto the counter, she chatted with the shop owner and selected more trinkets to buy. Then, purchases in hand, she strode purposely through the store and out the door.

The street was filled with restaurants, bars and high-end boutiques. Couples sat underneath umbrellas, chatting and eating. Tourists posed for pictures in front of cathedrals and museums, and police officers patrolled the area on foot. The sky was a magnificent blue, the brightest, most vivid shade. Church bells rang on the hour, opera music played in the distance and school children played soccer in the square.

"I'm going to get some gelato," Rafael said, gesturing to the small, quaint shop across the street. "Do you want some?"

Her face lit up and amusement twinkled in her almond-shaped eyes. "Do you even have to ask? I've been hooked on gelato since the first time you bought it for me!"

"What flavor do you want?"

"Surprise me."

Her innocent, good-girl smile made Rafael think wicked thoughts. He'd been fighting the desires of his flesh all afternoon, and he didn't know how much more of her teasing and flirting he could take without crossing the line.

Standing there, gazing at her, he noticed two things: the tiny freckles on her nose, and how plump and juicy her lips looked. He wanted to taste her, and imagined himself stroking her smooth skin.

"My cell phone's ringing!" Paris opened her handbag, and frantically searched around inside. Finding it, she sighed in relief, and typed in her password. "It was my dad. I better call him back. Do you mind?"

"No, not at all. I'll go grab the gelato."

"Great, because I could use a break." Paris sat down on a wrought-iron bench and dropped her shopping bags at her feet. "Ten minutes, and I'll be good to go. I promise."

Inside the store, Rafael placed his order and paid the cashier. His gaze strayed to the front window, and his smile faded. Paris was talking on her cell phone, and it was obvious the conversation was not going well. Her expression was somber, and her shoulders bent. Concerned, he grabbed their desserts and jogged back across the street.

"Fine, Dad, I'll do it. I don't have much of a choice, do I?"

Rafael sat down on the bench, and placed the cup holder beside him.

"I love you, too. Okay, I'll call you tomorrow."

Paris hurled her cell phone into her purse and raked a hand through her dark silky hair.

"What's wrong? You look upset."

"My father's assistant has been planning Excel Construction's charity gala, but now that she's off on medical leave he wants me to oversee the event."

"When is the gala?"

"Not until the end of March, but I don't have the time or energy to take on another project. I have enough on my plate as it is."

"Then hire a party planner and leave everything in their capable hands."

"You don't know my father," Paris muttered. "He's the stingiest millionaire you'll ever meet. If he finds out I spent thousands of dollars on a party planner he'll have a fit. He always does. No matter how minor the expense."

"There's nothing wrong with being money savvy, especially in this time of economic instability. The economy isn't what it used to be, and there's no telling when it will rebound," Rafael said thoughtfully.

"You only live once. Might as well live it up while you're here!" Paris retorted.

He raised an eyebrow. "Is that your personal philosophy?"

"Yeah, pretty much. My mom passed away when I was twelve years old, and I learned how fleeting happiness and success could be." Paris studied her French manicure, then twisted her long, delicate fingers together. "I've made a lot of mistakes, and I know my friends and family wish I wasn't so impulsive, but I have no regrets." She paused, then added, "The purpose of life is to live it, to taste adventure and excitement to the utmost and to reach out eagerly and without fear for newer and richer experiences."

"Wow, Paris, that's deep. I didn't realize you were such a poet."

"I'm not," she said, with a laugh. "I'm paraphrasing Eleanor Roosevelt!"

Chuckling, he picked up a cup of gelato and handed it to Paris. Their fingers touched, and the feel of her skin against his made his temperature soar. "I got you three scoops of dulce de leche," he said. *"Buon Appetito!"*

"It sounds decadent, and it smells delicious, too!" She dug her spoon into her gelato and put it in her mouth. Her eyelashes flicked and fluttered, and a sultry moan fell from her lips. "Oh, my, this is dreamy! What exactly is it?"

"Sweetened milk and caramel. I asked the clerk to add a splash of sherry, but she added *way* more than just a splash!"

"Great choice, Rafael. I think this is my new favorite flavor."

And I think you have the prettiest eyes I have ever seen.

"Looks like you have a new friend."

A small, brown dog was sitting at his feet, barking furiously. "Yeah, a hungry one who wants to steal my snack." Rafael reached into his backpack, took out his water bottle and poured some of the clear liquid into the puppy's mouth. "Good boy."

Paris gasped. "Oh, my, gosh, do you know what this reminds me of?"

"The freshman camping trip!" they shouted in unison.

"I almost died when that coyote snuck into your tent," she said with a laugh.

"You and me both. Thank God you had that chocolate bar in your backpack!"

Paris laughed until tears filled her eyes. "We had some great times, didn't we?"

"We sure did." Rafael couldn't control himself any longer and shocked them both by reaching out and caressing the length of her cheek. He inclined his head towards her, moving in close. He saw a nervous glint come across her face and watched her shift and shuffle around on the bench. It took everything in him not to crush his lips to her mouth. Still, after all these years, he felt connected to her, craved and desired her in ways he couldn't explain.

Paris fixed her gaze on him, and a shiver shot through his body. He felt his temperature spike, heard his pulse hammering in his ears. When Rafael saw something he wanted, whether in his personal life or in business he pursed it relentlessly, and right now Paris St. Clair was the object of his affection. His goal was twofold: to get her into his bed and to prove to that she'd made a mistake by dumping him years ago. "I'm having a great time. Are you?"

She nodded, but didn't speak.

"Nothing's changed. You're still the most fascinating woman I know, and I love spending time with you." Rafael was taken by her, attracted to her in every way and wondered if Paris felt the same way. But before he could ask her, she pulled away from him.

"We should go." She shot to her feet and grabbed her shopping bags. "There are a few more places I really want to see before it gets dark."

Disappointment flooded his body, but he slapped a smile on his face and stood in turn. "You're right, we should get going. We still haven't checked out any of the museums near Saint Mark's Square."

"You've seen one painting, you've seen them all, right?" she said wryly.

"Ok, so, what do you want to do next?"

"I'm dying to see the Doge's Palace and the Palazzo Dario."

Rafael studied her face for clues, tried to gauge if she was serious or joking and decided it had to be the latter. "You want to go to 'The House of No Return'?"

"Absolutely, it's on the top of my must-see list."

"But it's been cursed for centuries and historians are convinced it's haunted."

"I know. Isn't that crazy?" Paris laughed and shook her head. "I read all about it in my travel guide, but I find it hard to believe that such a striking piece of architecture is haunted. Too bad it isn't open to the public because I'd love to look around inside."

"I don't see why. The house is dark, creepy and condemned."

"I didn't come all the way to Venice to peruse art galleries and boutiques. I came to experience an exciting, new adventure." Gazing at him, Paris hitched a hand to her hip. "Haven't you ever felt the urge to do something wild and crazy?"

"No, never. I'm as by-the-book as they come."

"Come on, fess up. There must be something," she insisted, her tone full of sass. "What's the most fun you've ever had?"

The most fun I've ever had was making love to you.

"I'm waiting," she said in a singsong voice.

He thought hard, but drew a blank. "I'm just not a wild and crazy guy, I guess."

"What do you like to do in your free time?"

"Play with my dogs, exercise and watch documentaries."

"Wow! How exciting. You're a *real* party animal!"

"I enjoy my solitude," he said, feeling the need to defend himself. "I work eighty hours a week, and on Sundays I like to kick back and relax. What's wrong with that?"

"Nothing, if you're an eighty-year-old man…"

"What are you saying?"

"Live a little. You don't always have to be so serious and uptight…"

Rafael gulped. Uptight? *Is she calling me…boring?* He mentally stumbled over the word.

"Life is about having fun and trying new things, and that's exactly what I'm going to do." Paris took her travel guide out of her purse and then stared up at the bilingual street signs on the decorative lamp posts. "I'm going to the Doge's Palace. I'll see you later."

"I'll go with you," he said, touching her waist. "I don't want you to go alone."

"Are you sure?"

"I'm positive. It'll be great."

"Awesome," she said enthusiastically. "Let's go. It's only a few blocks from here."

Rafael swallowed a groan. *Lucky me.*

"Casanova was more than just a scheming womanizer," the tour guide said, his voice full of awe. "He was also a spy, a scam artist and one of the most fascinating men in Venetian history.…"

Paris tuned out the guide and admired the intricate carvings inside the small prison cell. The tour group was comprised of noisy travelers speaking a million different languages, and when they exited the dungeon, she was glad to see them go.

Paris looked up, caught Rafael watching her and broke into a shy smile. Goose bumps exploded across her arms, and tickled her flesh. Like fine wine, he just got better with age. He had killer sex appeal, and when he licked his lips,

Paris wondered what kind of damage his tongue could do between her legs. "I've never seen anything quite like this."

Rafael was standing outside of the cell, tapping his foot, clearly anxious to go. Paris didn't blame him. It turned out he was right. The dungeon was creepy, as dark as a hole in the ground, and if not for fear of looking like a scaredy cat she never would have descended into the depths of Doge's Palace.

"We better rejoin the group. I'd hate for us to get lost," Rafael said before taking her hand and leading her out of the dungeon and through the hallway. Paris heard the tour guide's loud, booming voice and knew the sightseeing group was nearby.

"Do you mind if we skip the rest of the tour?" she asked, rubbing her hands up and down her forearms. "This place is giving me the creeps!"

He gave her a one-arm hug. "You have nothing to worry about. I won't leave your side."

"Not even for the busty redhead?"

Rafael frowned. "What redhead?"

"Oh, come on, you mean you haven't noticed the chick in the fuchsia dress making eyes at you for the past forty-five minutes?"

"No, actually, I haven't. I've got a lot on my mind."

"Really? Want to talk about it?"

Raking a hand through his short dark hair, he shrugged and released a deep sigh. "I'm feeling for one of Cassandra's bridesmaids, but she won't give me the time of day."

His words were a crushing blow. Paris nodded in understanding, as if she was listening, but her thoughts were a million miles away. *How could Rafael be interested in someone else? Doesn't he feel the chemistry between us? The strong, mind-blowing attraction?*

Her mind returned to her favorite moments of the afternoon. Rafael was suave, chivalrous and smooth, and when he wasn't making her laugh, he was making her smile. Earlier, as they'd sat outside eating their gelato, she'd been so sure he was going to kiss her that she'd jumped to her feet in a state of panic.

Paris scolded herself for acting like a jittery fool back at Saint Mark's Square and vowed never to lose her cool again. Rafael was interested in someone else, and the suspense was killing her. All the bridesmaids were crushing hard on him, and the thought of him being intimate with someone else made her stomach lurch. "Who is it?" she blurted out, her curiosity finally getting the best of her. "It's one of the Wilson twins, isn't it?"

"I don't even know who they are!"

They laughed, and the tension in the air receded.

"She has gorgeous eyes, the sexiest pair of legs I've ever seen and a wicked sense of humor." Rafael stopped at the entrance of the palace and fixed his gaze on Paris. "We haven't seen each other in years, but I still find you incredibly attractive."

His words delighted her, filled her with pride.

"Our breakup was one of the worst things to ever happen to me," he confessed, in a soft, quiet voice. "And to this day I still don't know why you dumped me, Paris."

She lowered her head, shifted her tired, aching feet.

"Was it because of the stress you were under at home, or because you fell for that clown on the football team?"

Caught off guard by the question, she opened her eyes in surprise, and her mouth fell open. Standing at the entrance of the Doge's Palace was no place to have a heart-to-heart talk. But Rafael was opening up to her in a way he never had before, and Paris was desperate to clear the air once and for all. Maybe once they got everything out in the open she'd stop fantasizing about kissing him. At the thought, her nipples hardened under her dress. Banishing the image from her mind, she squared her shoulders and met his gaze head-on. "There was no one else."

"You started dating another guy a few weeks after our breakup."

Paris held up an index finger. "We went on one date. That's it."

"That's not what I heard."

"Why does it matter? It's not like you stayed home lamenting our breakup. As I recall, you hit the clubs pretty hard that summer."

"I had to do something to get over losing you."

"Rafael, I had to break things off with you. My dad gave me no choice."

Rafael regarded her intently.

"My father went ballistic when he found out my sister was pregnant and had dropped out of college," Paris explained, shivering at the bittersweet memory of that Sunday afternoon. "I think he was scared of me becoming a teenage mother, too. He had high hopes for me, and he didn't want you messing up my plans."

"Is that what he said?"

Paris shook her head. "No, but he told me if I didn't break up with you and focus on my studies he'd cut me off financially, and at nineteen I was in no position to take care of myself."

The expression on Rafael's face broke her heart. Seeing the hurt in his eyes made Paris regret the way she'd treated him in the past. She wanted to apologize, to tell him how much she'd loved him, but couldn't bring herself to say the words. Not after fifteen long years apart. They'd moved on, had other relationships, and Paris didn't want him to think she'd been pining over him for almost two decades.

"Why didn't you tell me the truth?" he asked.

"I didn't know how to."

Rafael nodded. "I understand, and I appreciate your honesty now."

"And, for the record, I went out with that football player because his parents and my dad are good friends. Not because I liked him."

Seconds passed, and the tension grew thicker than smoke.

The sound of Paris's ring tone broke the silence.

"It's Cassandra," she said, reading her latest text message. "And she's not happy. We better go. The wedding rehearsal starts at six, and if I'm late she'll kill me!"

Rafael checked his wristwatch. "The church isn't far from here, but we'll have to take a vaporetto to get there on time."

"A vaporetto? What's that?"

"A motorized boat. They work just like a city bus except they stop at docks and never get flat tires," he joked, leading her out the museum doors.

Outside, they bought tickets at a tiny white booth and headed to the nearest dock. Minutes later, they boarded a water taxi and found seats at the rear. The air was warm, the breeze strong and the sky was filled with hundreds of faint stars.

"Here, take my coat."

"No, thank you, I'm not cold."

Rafael took off his jacket and draped it over her arms, anyway. "You have to cover your shoulders or you'll be turned away at the church."

"Oh, thanks, I had no idea."

Within minutes, they arrived at the breathtaking fifteenth-century cathedral. When Paris spotted Julietta pacing in front of the church, she strangled a groan.

"I'll see you back at the villa."

Paris gestured to the church. "You're not coming inside?"

"No, I have tons of work to do, and I still have to write a speech for the bride and groom. Tomorrow is the big day, and I don't want to let them down."

"That's right. You're the master of ceremonies. Are you nervous?"

"No," he said confidently, licking his lips. "I think it's going to be fun and good practice for my brother's weddings next year."

"I guess I'll see you tomorrow, then."

"Don't forget to save me a dance." Rafael gave her shoulders an affectionate squeeze while juggling their bags from shopping and then dropped a kiss on her cheek. "Good night, Paris," he said as he handed over her belongings.

Long after he walked away, Paris stood on the street, thinking about him and all the fun they'd had that afternoon. Closing her eyes, she buried her face in his jacket and inhaled the scent of his fragrant cologne. She was so aroused by his chaste kiss, her body was inflamed with desire. She craved more, could almost feel his hands stroking and caressing her flesh, and struggled to answer the question plaguing her thoughts. *How am I supposed to resist a man whose smile makes me weak and whose touch leaves me breathless?*

Chapter 7

Paris sat at the head table inside the grand ballroom at the Hotel Excelsior Venice, watching the bride and groom waltz around the dance floor. She'd never seen a couple more in love. The wedding ceremony had been touching, so heartfelt it had moved her to tears. Deep, choking sobs had raked her body as she'd listened to Stefano recite his handwritten vows. Crying was completely out of character, something Paris never did, but standing at the altar with two people who deeply loved each other made her secretly long to have someone special in her life. Someone who'd support her and be there for her at the end of a long, stressful day.

As Paris dabbed at her cheeks, something truly remarkable had happened. She'd caught sight of Rafael sitting in the first pew, and when their eyes met she'd felt an overwhelming sense of peace, a calm she'd never known.

He was working the hell out of his black tuxedo and eye-catching blue vest, but it was the sympathetic expression on his handsome face that had made her heart pitter-patter.

The rest of the ceremony went off without a hitch, and it turned out Cassandra was right about Rafael. He was more charismatic than a politician, and his quiet confidence was a turn-on. During dinner he entertained guests with hilarious tales about Stefano, recited poetry and even serenaded the bride.

Paris picked up the chocolate truffle on her plate, popped it in her mouth and savored the sweet, rich taste. As she ate, she admired the elaborate centerpieces on the table. Silver ribbons hung from the ceiling, potted candles emitted a soft, pink light, and long-stemmed roses filled the air with an intoxicating fragrance. Paris felt as if she was in an enchanted wonderland and marveled at the size and grandeur of the soaring ice sculptures and eight-tier wedding cake.

Searching the room for Rafael, she found him standing at the champagne bar with Julietta. Paris's eyes narrowed. For some reason, seeing them together made her green with envy. The blonde had been nipping at his heels since he'd arrived at the villa three days earlier, and as Paris watched them on the sly she couldn't help wondering if the would-be model was making any progress. Yesterday, while shopping, Rafael had said he wasn't interested in Julietta, but Paris didn't believe him for a second. *Of course he's into Julietta,* her conscience argued. *She young and perky and eager to please!*

Paris tore her gaze away from the bar. Smiling to herself, she stroked the delicate rose petals of the bride's bouquet. Too competitive to lose, she'd fought off the other bridesmaids and the groom's cousins to catch the bouquet. And when Paris was declared the winner, she'd danced around the grand ballroom, posing for pictures with her sweet-smelling prize.

"All right, guys, it's your turn!" Stefano said, waving the bride's garter in the air.

Reluctantly, all the bachelors in the audience stood and ambled out onto the dance floor. Paris watched, amused, as Cassandra grabbed Rafael's hand, then dragged him to his feet and through the room as if he were an errant child. He stood behind the sour-faced group, staring down at his cell phone, seemingly bored.

"Ready, fellas?" Stefano flashed a mischievous grin. "Ready or not, here it comes!"

He twirled the garter around on his finger and then tossed it over his shoulder. It dropped on the floor, and the men nearby scattered in all directions.

Guests cracked up.

"Rafael won!" Cassandra scooped up her frilly lace garter, tucked it inside Rafael's front pocket and gave him a peck on the cheek. "Congratulations!"

Paris knew what was coming next, but before she could jump to her feet and make a run for it Cassandra grabbed the microphone out of the DJ's hand and said, "Paris St. Clair, get down here and come bust a move with your future husband!"

Cheers exploded across the room. Everyone was smiling and laughing—everyone except Julietta. The groom's cousin was shooting evil daggers at her, so Paris shot them right back. *Who does she think she is?*

Ignoring her new blonde nemesis, she rose gracefully from her chair and carefully descended the short staircase. Drawing upon what she'd learned in etiquette class way back when, she raised her chin, pinned her shoulders back and sucked in her stomach. Each step Paris took hurt like hell, and all she could think about was soaking her tired feet in a bowl of Epsom salts later that night.

The moment Paris heard the opening bars of her favorite Backstreet Boys song she knew she'd been set up. And the cheeky grin on her best friend's face confirmed it. Paris wanted to smack Cassandra for tricking her, but when Rafael slid his arms around her waist, her anger evaporated into thin air. His touch was magic, and his dark, smoldering gaze made her feel sexier than a model frolicking on the beach.

They swayed to the beat of the music, moved their hands and legs in perfect sync. It was hard not to get lost in his eyes, impossible not to be swept up in the moment. His slow, sensual dancing aroused her and caused explicit thoughts to flood her mind. Turned on, she fought to control the tingling sensation between her legs. Paris was trembling, hot all over, and her entire body was damp with sweat. Her throat was bone dry, and she was so nervous she couldn't think of anything smart or interesting to say.

She knew everyone was watching them, could feel the heat of their stares, but she refused to let her nerves get the best of her. Swallowing hard, she searched the crowd for a friendly face. The bride and groom waved, and a laugh fell from her lips. Seeing Cassandra and Stefano wrapped in each other's arms made Paris smile. She hadn't seen her friend this happy in years, and she was thrilled that her girlfriend had finally found true love.

"Are you having a good time?"

The sound of Rafael's deep voice instantly seized her attention and sent ripples of pleasure down her spine. "Of course," she said with a nod. "I'm a foodie with a bottomless stomach, and the selection was to die for."

"I couldn't help but notice you tonight." Desire blazed in his eyes, warmed his light brown skin. "You look sensational, *and* you made four trips to the dessert station."

Paris pressed a finger to her lips and glanced around playfully. "Don't tell anyone, but I have chocolate biscotti hidden inside my purse!"

"I hate to brag, but I've been told my orange-pecan biscotti ranks right up there with the best of them," he said, his voice oh so smooth. "Next time you're in Washington I'd love to make you an authentic Italian meal."

"You cook?"

"Of course, I'm a Morretti!" Rafael chuckled. "My father taught me and my brothers how to cook at a very young age, and we can all throw down in the kitchen. But you don't have to take my word for it. I'll show you."

Her mind went blank and her heart swooned. *Good God, is he trying to seduce me?*

"I frequently fly to Atlanta for business, so we can definitely make it happen…."

He spoke in a low, husky whisper, one intended to arouse and seduce. He caressed her hips slowly as they moved to the music. His stroke set her body on fire, causing her to yearn for French kisses and passionate lovemaking. Paris recalled their first date, and all her feelings and emotions for Rafael came rushing back.

"When's a good time for you?"

"I'll, um, have to get back to you." She wouldn't, of course, but Rafael didn't need to know the truth. Or that she'd be in Washington next Friday to prepare for the Women's Business Expo. Being the keynote speaker at the sold-out conference was an incredible honor, and Paris needed to be more focused than ever. Rafael was her weakness, the ultimate distraction, but Paris was too smart to act on her feelings. *The last time I let someone get close to me he betrayed my trust, and I'd rather be alone for the rest of my life than get hurt by another charming, charismatic man.*

"I'm going to hold you to that," he said, tightening his arm around her waist. "It's not often I meet a woman of your caliber, and I'd be honored to take you out on a *second* first date."

Paris concealed a smile. She didn't know how he did it. He had the ability to connect with people, no matter how old or young they were, no matter their race or gender. For the past three hours she'd watched in awe as Rafael worked his charms on everyone in the grand ballroom. She admired his intelligence and loved how his eyes twinkled whenever he teased her.

"I think you're an incredible woman, and I hope this is the start of a great friendship."

I hope this is the start of a great friendship? Paris almost laughed out loud, but caught herself in the nick of time. *I can't be friends with you. You're a charmer and if I wasn't so afraid of you breaking my heart, I'd do you right here, right now!*

Paris maneuvered the conversation to a safer, less personal subject and spoke with excitement about her company's charity gala in Washington, D.C. "Soldier's Angels is a remarkable charity, and I'm hoping to raise a million dollars for the brave men and women who need this vital organization."

"I'll send a generous donation in your name."

"If you attend the event, I'll save you a dance," she said, with a cheeky smile.

"Black-tie events aren't really my thing," he confessed. "I'm a numbers guy so I leave the partying and schmoozing to my father and Nicco."

The music ended, but Rafael pulled her closer to his chest.

"Is it true you spent the morning doing everyone's hair and makeup?"

"Not everyone," Paris said. "Just the girls in the bridal party."

"You make it sound like it's no big deal, but I bet it was a lot of work."

"The stylist Cassandra booked for the wedding never showed up, and when she started crying I knew I had to do something, so I grabbed my curling iron and got down to work."

"You're very talented."

And you're very sexy!

"There's nothing worse than wasted potential, and it would be a shame to spend your life doing something you're not passionate about."

His words gave her something to think about. Was he

right? Was she talented enough to run her own beauty salon, or would she fall flat on her face again?

Paris danced with Rafael for the next hour, and was having so much fun laughing and joking with him she forgot all about her tired, aching feet. "This DJ is off the chain!" Waving her hands in the air, she swiveled her hips to the loud, infectious beat. "I can't believe he's playing The Fugees. I haven't heard this song in years!"

"It takes me way back—"

"All the way back to the U of W's winter ball our freshman year?" Paris asked, with a coy smile.

"I had an amazing time that night."

"What was your favorite part?"

Rafael lowered his mouth to her ear. "Making love to you in the backseat of the limo."

"I'm surprised you remember."

"How could I forget? You rocked my world that night."

His words gave her a rush. The air was thick, saturated with the scent of his desire and charged with electricity. Their connection was strong, still as powerful as ever, and all Paris could think about was kissing him. The strength of his gaze and the soulful, sensuous music playing in the background only heightened her need.

"May I cut in?"

Paris turned, saw Julietta standing behind her and stared her down.

"Now's not a good time." Rafael had a cold, grim look on his face, but he spoke in a soft tone.

"But you promised me a dance, and I've been waiting for over an hour."

"Then go bust a move with someone else."

"You guys are hilarious," Paris quipped. "You bicker like an old married couple!"

The blonde wore a triumphant smile. "See, Rafael, I told you! I'm not the only one who thinks we're a great match."

"I need a drink," Paris said, turning to walk away.

Rafael grabbed her arm and pulled her to his side. "Hold on, I'm coming with you."

"You are?"

"Of course. You're one hell of a dancer, and I worked up quite a sweat trying to keep up with you." He led her across the room and sighed in relief when they reached the champagne bar. "Do me a favor. The next time you see Julietta coming, tell me to run!"

Paris giggled. Couldn't help it. Men who could make her laugh were hard to come by, but Rafael had been making her giggle all night.

"What would you like to drink?"

"Champagne, please."

Rafael spoke to the bartender in Italian, and Paris fanned a hand in front of her face. *It's bad enough he's tall, dark and dreamy. Does he have to sound sexy, too?*

"When are you heading back to the States?"

"Bright and early tomorrow morning." Paris took the goblet he offered her and tasted her drink. It helped take the edge off her nerves. "I have a meeting in the afternoon that I can't afford to miss. I do wish I could stay in Venice a few more days, though. But there are clients to meet, deals to close and money to be made."

"Amen to that!"

They laughed and clinked glasses.

"I need to use the powder room, so if I don't see you again tonight have a safe trip back to the States. Oh, and Happy New Year!"

"Well, can I have your number? We've had such a great time reconnecting and I'd like us to keep in touch."

Paris loved the idea of seeing Rafael again, but tempered her excitement. Their attraction was stronger than ever, and she feared what would happen if they renewed their relationship. "Really? But we're both insanely busy."

"It's a ninety-minute flight from Washington to Atlanta, and my family is fortunate enough to have our own plane," he said, with a hint of pride in his voice. "We can see each other as often as you'd like, and it won't cost you a dime."

"Rafael, I'm not looking for anything serious."

"Me, neither. A few more dinner dates and slow dances should suffice."

His grin was dangerous, and so were his dark, piercing eyes.

"Next time I'm in Washington I'll look you up. How's that?"

His smile fell away. "It sounds like you're giving me the brush-off."

"Why would I do that?"

"Because you're scared of history repeating itself."

Surprised and confused, she frowned and folded her arms. *What's* that *supposed to mean? Is Rafael trying to imply that I was sprung back in the day? That I was as desperate as Julietta?*

The music faded and a hush fell over the room.

"I'd like to call the Morretti brothers up to the podium," the DJ said.

"Hang tight, okay?" Rafael kissed her cheek, and affectionately squeezed her shoulder. "I'll be back in a couple minutes."

The air was filled with excitement, and the whistles and applause were deafening.

"Cassandra, you're the best thing to ever happen to Stefano, and if he *ever* steps out of line, just let me know and I'll straighten him out," Nicco said, with a rueful smile.

Demetri stole the microphone and pointed a finger at his chest. "Call me first! He's been scared of me since the tenth grade, and I *still* outweigh him by forty pounds!"

Guests hooted and hollered.

"In a few minutes we'll be going outside to watch a

spectacular fireworks display, but before we do I'd like to make one last toast to the bride and groom." Rafael raised his silver goblet in the air and spoke in a loud, clear voice. "I hope your marriage is filled with unspeakable joy and happiness, and may those of us who haven't found our soul mates be fortunate enough to find a love as strong as yours...."

Paris felt the tears coming and dabbed at her eyes with her fingertips. Rafael spoke with such passion and conviction the crowd gave him a standing ovation.

And no one cheered louder or longer than she did.

Chapter 8

"Where are you rushing off to, pretty lady? I have big plans for you tonight."

Paris groaned and dropped her gaze to the sleek marble floor. Glancing over her shoulder confirmed it was the groom's uncle strutting toward her with lust in his eyes. Paris was standing in the lobby of the Hotel Excelsior, had been for several minutes while wondering why the elevator was taking forever to reach the main floor. And why Stefano's uncle was pestering her.

"Where have you been? I've been looking all over for you."

"Bye, Luigi. See you around."

He growled and licked his dry, thin lips.

Yuck. Paris didn't get it. How could someone as suave and well-bred as Stefano have such a sleazy uncle? Why couldn't he be more like Rafael and less of a horndog? A picture of Raphael popped into her mind, but she pushed the image aside and faced her tormentor. Stefano's uncle smelled faintly of vodka and cheap cologne. He was invading her personal space, standing too close for her liking, and she hated the way he was ogling her cleavage.

"You're working the hell out of that dress." Grunting, he patted his protruding belly with gusto. "You look so tasty tonight I could sop you up with a biscuit!"

Ignoring him, Paris frantically jabbed the up button and tapped her foot impatiently. Cheers and laughter rang out behind her. The lobby was loud, filled with well-dressed guests and spirited conversation. Paris was enjoying her stay at the hotel with the spectacular view of the Grand Canal. She had already decided the next time she was in Venice she would definitely be paying Hotel Excelsior another visit.

Who knows? Maybe Rafael will join me.

At the thought, her heart skipped a beat. They'd had fun sightseeing yesterday and had flirted with each other throughout the wedding reception, but that didn't mean Paris wanted to rekindle their romance. She didn't.

Liar, jeered her conscience. *You want him bad, and you know it!*

"The bridal party and some of the out-of-town guests are going to The Zone nightclub, and I want you to be the lucky lady on my arm," Luigi said, his tone full of bravado. "We have some unfinished business to discuss, *and* some dirty dancing to do."

Paris wanted to smack the lewd grin off his face, but exercised restraint. She was anxious to return to her suite, and envisioned herself stretched out in the Jacuzzi tub, eating fruit and listening to cool jazz. *Now if I could only get rid of Stefano's uncle without having to use the can of mace in my purse, life would be golden!*

"Thanks, but I'm not interested."

"Of course you are."

Is he deaf, or just hard of hearing? Paris had plans to go upstairs to her plush, sixth-floor suite, and nothing was going to stop her. She'd toasted the bride and groom, smiled for so many pictures her jaw hurt and fulfilled all of her maid-of-honor duties. And although she wished she didn't have to wake up at the crack of dawn for her 7:00 a.m. flight, she decided to look on the bright side. She'd had a wonderful time in Venice with her girlfriends, *and* reconnected with Rafael. *Hopefully, he'll be at the Excel*

Construction charity gala in March, she thought, excited by the prospect of seeing him again soon.

"I'll take you to the party bus. It's waiting just outside."

Paris patted back a yawn and wrapped her arms around her shoulders. "I'm exhausted. It's been a long day and the only place I want to go is to my suite."

"Do you want some company?"

"Do you want a knuckle sandwich?"

He popped his shirt collar. "Quit playing hard to get. You know you want me."

Paris cracked up, laughing so hard that tears began to slide down her cheeks.

Rafael found Paris standing in the lobby, clutching her sides and laughing hysterically. He didn't like the way Luigi was ogling her, found his sneer disrespectful and struggled to control his temper. Paris looked smokin' hot in her silver gown and high heels but that didn't give Luigi—a three-time loser with a string of ex-wives—the right to harass her.

"What's up?" Rafael asked, unable to hide his disdain. "I hope I'm not interrupting anything."

"You are. I'm talking to my girl, so kick rocks, Rafael."

Paris pursed her moist, red lips. Her expression was one of pure shock, and her hands were balled into fists, like a boxer ready to fight. "Your girl? Luigi, please. You've got to be kidding, because we both know I'm *way* too much woman for you."

A grin curved Rafael's lips. *I couldn't have said it better myself.*

The elevator chimed, and several women with big hair, fake eyelashes and short dresses sashayed out. The trio gave him the once-over, then oohed like a game show studio audience. But Rafael pretended they weren't there. He kept his eyes on Paris, admiring her elegant, glamorous look. On the surface he appeared cool, like the smart, accomplished businessman he was, but inside he was a ball of nerves. And he had a hard-on the size of a two-by-four threatening to explode out of his pants.

"Good night, fellas." Paris strode into the elevator and waved. "Happy New Year!"

As the doors started to close, Rafael slid inside the metal box, then pressed the button for the twentieth floor. "Are you okay?" he asked, gesturing to her leg. "It looks like you're favoring your left foot."

Paris wore a sheepish smile. "I am. I love my Louboutins, but they're killing me!"

"Then take them off."

"Good idea." She kicked off her shoes, sighed in relief and scooped them up off the floor. "Are you going to the nightclub with the group?"

"Yeah, unfortunately. I'm just going upstairs to change."

"Julietta finally wore you down, huh?" Paris took her key card out of her purse and shot him a coy smile. "Let me guess. She made you an offer you just couldn't refuse."

"No, Angela and Jariah told me if I didn't come they'd create a profile for me online, and nothing scares me more than that!"

The elevator stopped on the sixth floor and the doors slid open. Rafael didn't know what came over him, but he scooped Paris up in his arms and held her close to his chest.

"Rafael, what are you doing? Put me down!"

He took a good, hard look at her, inhaling her sweet, floral scent. Her hair was swept up in a chic bun, her eyes shimmered with bronze glitter and diamond hoops dangled from her ears. Her beauty knocked the wind out of him, and it took every ounce of his self-control not to devour her lips and ravish her body. "I can't stand to see you limp."

"I'm fine, really. I can walk."

"Then humor me," he said with a shrug. "I get a kick

out of sweeping beautiful women off their feet, and you're a vision of loveliness tonight."

"I'm heavier than I look. I don't want you to hurt yourself."

"Don't worry, I got you." Standing in the hallway, holding Paris in his arms, Rafael realized he wasn't much better than Stefano's uncle. He'd crossed the line, fell victim to his desires, but when it came to his first love his body had a mind of its own. Her smile, her walk and the poise and grace she embodied drew him to her. Rafael suspected that would never change.

"I can't believe you're carrying me to my suite," Paris said, shaking her head in disbelief. "This reminds me of the day I twisted my ankle playing coed volleyball. You carried me all the way to the health clinic and never once complained."

"That's what real men do. They take care of the women they love."

Her breathing sped up and her eyes brightened.

Rafael could feel the electricity crackling between them, but kept his head *and* his body in check. He thought back on the fun they'd had tonight, laughing and joking around like they used to but he didn't want to push his luck or get smacked upside the head for trying to kiss her.

"Make a left and head straight down the hall," she said.

As Rafael carried her along the corridor, a fragrant scent filled the air, one that made his mouth water and his stomach grumble. Though it couldn't compare to the sweetness of the woman he was holding in his arms.

"This is my suite," she called out. "Thanks for the lift."

Carefully, he set her down and stepped aside. "It was my pleasure."

Paris unlocked the door, then cast a glance over her shoulder. Amusement shone in her eyes and her lips held a coy smirk. "Do you want to come inside for a drink?"

"I better not."

Her smile fell away. "Why not? You used to love my dirty martinis."

"You've had a lot to drink tonight, and I don't want to take advantage of you."

"Who's to say I won't be the one taking advantage of *you?*"

His erection strained against his tuxedo pants, threatened to break free of his zipper. All his life he'd been criticized by his friends and brothers for being boring, for playing it safe, but tonight Rafael wanted to break every rule in the book. He saw the twinkle in her eyes, heard the thick huskiness of her voice and realized his first love had the same thought in mind. He'd never wanted anyone more, but refrained from quickly pulling her into his arms and crushing his mouth against hers. *There's nothing worse than a desperate man, so play it cool and don't rush her.*

"Join me for a nightcap." Meeting his gaze, Paris boldly stepped forward and draped her arms around his neck. "I can't think of a better way to ring in the New Year. Can you?"

Paris knew the kiss was coming and had been craving it since the moment she'd first spotted Rafael three days earlier. But she was still blown away by the intensity and ferocity of it. Her body hummed and throbbed, vibrated and quivered at his touch. Kissing him was like coming home, as natural as breathing. His mouth was sweet, flavored with champagne and intoxicating. One kiss and she was hooked, hungry and desperate for more.

"You taste even better than I remember," he said, in a guttural tone.

Lips locked, their bodies pressed flat against each other, they stumbled inside the suite and collapsed against the door. His lips were made for kissing, for licking and sucking, and Paris couldn't get enough of his mouth. His hands ran through her hair, then caressed her neck and shoulders. Salsa dancing, her new vicarious pleasure, helped her stay fit, relieved stress and bolstered her confidence, but nothing made Paris feel sexier than being in Rafael's arms.

Inhaling his scent, she relished the feel of his touch and the pleasure of his kiss. His lips felt oh so good, and tasted even better.

The kiss took on a life of its own, growing more intense with each flick of his tongue. Her desire for Rafael was insatiable, more powerful than any drug. They pawed and fondled each other for what felt like hours. It was the hottest foreplay she'd ever had, and they were still dressed.

Anxious to stroke and taste his physique, she shrugged his jacket down his shoulders and let it fall to the floor. She whipped off his shirt, undid his tie and took off his pants in the blink of an eye. Baby-fine hair sprinkled his upper chest, his stomach was as flat as a surfboard and his skin was smooth to the touch. He was every woman's dream, and Paris couldn't wait to feel him inside her.

Overcome with longing, she sprayed kisses along his collarbone and over his pecs and biceps. Tasting and touching him intensified her need. Paris felt lost, out of it, as if she were in another world. It was a struggle to stay present, in the moment, when all she could think about was throwing him to the floor, climbing onto his lap and riding him until he said *her* name.

Cradling his head in her hands, she stroked his ears, his neck and his shoulders. Pressing her hips against his, she slowly massaged his erection with her pelvis. The champagne she'd had at the wedding reception brought out her boldness. Paris reached between Rafael's legs and seized his length. He was well-endowed, long and thick, and as she worked her fingers up and down his shaft her nipples hardened under her dress.

Rafael's cell phone rang, and Paris froze. She feared their intimate party for two was about to end abruptly and imagined herself tossing his clothes out the balcony window to prevent him from leaving.

"Aren't you going to answer your phone?"

"Ignore it," he said, flashing a grin. "It's just Nicco."

Paris felt a twinge of guilt and wondered if Rafael was having second thoughts about being with her. Her doubts grew and her desire fizzled. "You're supposed to be going clubbing with your brothers tonight. Won't they be disappointed if you blow them off?"

"Don't know. Don't care."

"Of course you do," she argued. "They're your family."

"True, but you're the sexiest woman in Venice and I'd rather be here with you than in a smoky nightclub with my brothers and their fiancées."

"I'm flattered."

Rafael nipped at her earlobe and cupped her ass in his hands. "I aim to please."

His low raspy voice aroused her, causing her breath to catch on a moan.

"This dress is in my way," he grumbled. "It needs to go. *Now.*"

Paris felt him fumbling for the zipper of her gown and gasped when she heard the fabric ripping. "Rafael, stop!" she shrieked, bracing her hands against his muscled chest. "This is a Badgley Mischka gown, and it cost five grand!"

"And?" Moonlight cast a faint glow inside the suite and illuminated the amused expression on his lean, chiseled face. "I can afford to buy you the entire collection, and anything else your heart desires. You know that."

"When did you get so smug?"

He pinned her hands high above her head. "When you lured me inside your suite."

"Is that what happened?"

"Isn't it?"

Paris unzipped her dress, watched it fall to the floor in a glitzy heap and kicked it aside. Standing in front of Rafael in just her jewelry made her feel confident, sexier than ever. Her alcohol-induced buzz was bringing out her inner sex kitten, a side she never knew she had, but wanted to discover.

"You're not wearing any panties."

His breath tickled her ears and the lips between her legs. "Are you disappointed?"

Rafael gave a slow nod. "I wanted to rip them off."

"Next time."

Crushing his lips to her mouth, he flicked and licked her tongue with his own. His hands rode up her thighs, stroked her hips and stomach. Moans and groans fell from her lips, becoming a slow, erotic chant. Her heart was beating fast, out of control, and she felt exhilarated, as if she was floating in the evening sky.

The room spun at a dizzying speed. Something primal came over her, something so strong and powerful she could hardly breathe. Her body shivered and trembled.

Her temperature climbed, shot through the roof like a rocket. Paris feared she was going to black out, wondered if it was possible for a woman to die of pleasure. Rafael was the world's greatest kisser, always had been. He did things with his lips and tongue that should be illegal. Tremors stabbed her flesh, zigzagged down her spine and legs. *I can't take any more…. This is all too much and we haven't even had sex yet!*

Feeling hot way down below, as if her clit was on fire, she felt her limbs grow heavy and her body go weak. Paris loved taking charge in the bedroom and wasn't afraid to speak her mind, but Rafael didn't need any pointers. It was as if they were still in college, as if fifteen years hadn't passed since they'd last seen each other.

His touch was electrifying, the best thing that had ever happened to her body. Her urges grew stronger, more frenzied and intense. Paris needed him now, ached to feel him inside her, and what she did next shocked them both. She took his index finger, licked it like a lollipop and then guided it between her thighs. Hooking a leg around his waist, she thrust her hips forward, invited him to feel her wetness.

To give him better access to her clit, Paris arched her spine and spread herself wide open. He moved his fingers in and out, back and forth, from side to delicious side. Tingles danced up her thighs and warmed her throbbing, aching clit. Gripping his forearm to hold him in place, she rode his fingers hard and fast, with all the lust and desire pulsing through her veins.

Electric shocks pricked her flesh, stabbed and tickled her clit. Pleasure built, rose to unimaginable heights. Throwing her head back in ecstasy, Paris pressed her eyes shut and rode out the wave that claimed her body. Her climax was explosive, the most powerful orgasm she'd ever had, and several seconds passed before her feet touched the ground.

Hot and desperate for more, she seized his erection and stroked it over the lips between her thighs. Rafael groaned as if tormented, then pulled away. "We can't do this...."

Paris blinked, slowly surfaced from her haze. It was hard to focus, impossible to listen to what he was saying. Rafael was naked, standing before her in all his masculine glory with a long, thick erection. His length was unbelievable, jaw-dropping, and all Paris could think about was riding all eight inches.

"Angel eyes, we have to stop. I don't have any protection on me."

Paris smiled, and her heart danced inside her chest.

Hearing Rafael use her old pet name made her want him even more. "I'm on the pill, and I've never had an STD."

"Me neither, but—"

"You know me, Rafael. You can trust me."

He paused and then shook his head. "There's a convenience store a few blocks from here. I'll be back before you know it."

Paris locked her arms around his neck. For good measure, she cradled his head in her hands and made sweet, sensuous love to his mouth. "You're not going anywhere," she whispered, scattering soft kisses along his jawline. "You're staying here with me, and that's that."

A grin lit his eyes. "When did you get so feisty?"

"When you ripped off my designer gown."

Rafael chuckled.

She sucked his earlobe into her mouth, showing him what he'd be missing if he ditched her. "Don't go. I need you right here, right now...."

A wild, crazed expression darkened his handsome face.

He gripped her hips, drove powerfully inside her, thrust in and out at a furious, frantic speed. His length consumed and possessed her. Rafael gave her everything he had, everything she needed. His stroke pushed her to the edge of delirium. Every grind shook her to the core. Their lovemaking was everything she was looking for—erotic, sensuous and passionate—and Paris didn't want it to ever end.

Rafael tickled her ear with his tongue, licked and nibbled as if it was a candy cane, and she all but lost her mind. Savage grunts and groans exploded from her mouth, and she bucked against him like an out-of-control mare.

To stop from crying out and waking up everyone on the sixth floor, Paris clamped her lips together and buried her face in his chest. The tingling sensation in her feet coursed up her legs and shot straight to her core. Spasms caused her muscles to tense, her G-spot to tingle and throb. Rafael had the best sexual technique known to man, and his moves were erotic. But what impressed her most was his selflessness. All he cared about was pleasing her, and she adored him for it. He was in a league of his own, and no one would ever take his place in her heart.

Rafael mashed her breasts together, and when he flicked his tongue over each erect nipple, an explosion erupted between Paris's legs. She couldn't think, lost all sense of time and place. Her body felt weightless, and she was quivering uncontrollably. Her breath came in short, quick gasps and her heartbeat drummed in her ears. Rafael clutched her hips and thrust so deep inside her she shuddered and climaxed. One orgasm followed another, and soon she lost count of how many times she'd come.

Seconds passed before the room stopped spinning. The fragrance of their lovemaking was intoxicating, a sweet aroma that filled every inch of her posh, sixth-floor suite. Paris opened her eyes, took one look at Rafael and decided the businessman with the brilliant mind and quiet demeanor was the sexiest man on the face of the earth. He'd brought her to orgasm in a way no one had before, and although they'd just finished, Paris was ready for rounds two, three and four. *Damn,* she thought, blowing out a deep breath.

"That was incredible," Rafael exclaimed, lowering her to the ground.

"I bet you say that to all your lovers."

He shook his head and cupped her chin in his palm. His gaze was deadly, filled with such passion and heat, it consumed her. "Not everyone. Just you."

He spoke softly to her, in a quiet, subdued voice, but Paris heard his desire, his hunger. "You're a woman who isn't afraid to take control of her pleasure. I like that."

"And I like the way you make me feel. Your stroke is out of this world."

Amusement twinkled in his eyes. "Out of this world, huh?"

"You've always been a great lover, but that was toe-curling, head-spinning, mind-blowing good, and I can't wait for round two."

"Why wait when there's plenty more where that came from?"

Chapter 9

"Pick up, dammit." Rafael paced inside the master bedroom of suite 608 in nothing but his black boxer briefs, cursing and mumbling in Italian. He glanced at the bedside clock, saw that it was nine o'clock and hoped luck was on his side. The bride and groom were leaving for their honeymoon at noon, and he had to speak to Stefano before the newlyweds boarded their flight for the Galapagos Islands. Rafael had a score to settle with Paris, and it couldn't wait.

At the thought of the captivating beauty who'd given him the best sex of his life, then promptly skipped town, his hands clenched into tight fists. Making love to Paris was supposed to alleviate his stress, and his growing anxiety about the future, but he'd never felt more alone. He was confused, out of sorts, and couldn't handle his emotions. Rafael felt a twinge in his heart, a pain that burned and throbbed inside the walls of his chest, and wondered what he'd done to deserve being used and ditched. He'd woke up an hour earlier, expecting to see Paris lying in bed beside him, but she was nowhere to be found. He'd never been rejected by a woman before, especially after a passionate sexual encounter, and didn't like the feeling.

His gaze bounced aimlessly around the suite. He felt strange being there without Paris, but didn't want to leave until he knew exactly where she was. But phone calls to the hotel spa, gym and restaurant confirmed his worst fear: she was gone. His first thought was to call her, but he didn't have her cell phone number. And since the front desk clerk wouldn't give it to him, tracking his best friend down was his only other option.

The call went straight to voice mail, and Rafael did what he'd done three times before: he hung up and hit Redial. Sunshine streamed in through the balcony doors, but the warmth did nothing to improve his mood. He was pissed, and he couldn't wait to get his hands on Paris Sex-Him-and-Leave-Him St. Clair. She'd sexed him in a hundred different ways, then disappeared like a thief in the night. *Who does that?*

Rafael dropped down onto the chocolate-brown armchair, rested his cell phone on the side table and massaged his tired, aching shoulder muscles. Paris had worked him over real good last night, done things to him in bed that blew his mind. He'd woken up that morning hungry for more, only to find her gone, and her betrayal stung like hell.

As he shrugged on his wrinkled dress shirt and tuxedo pants, he spotted something shiny peeking out from underneath the king-size bed. Rafael bent down, lifted the blanket and picked up the diamond necklace. Holding it in his hands, he studied the delicate, heart-shaped locket. *No way,* he told himself, adamantly shaking his head. *This isn't it. It can't be....*

Rafael turned the pendant over, saw the inscription R.M.'s Girl, and knew it was the necklace he'd bought Paris for her twentieth birthday, the one he'd scrimped and saved to buy. Questions flooded his mind. Why had she kept the necklace all these years? Had she been wearing it all weekend? Why hadn't he recognized it before?

Because you were too busy drooling over her curves, his conscience reminded him.

Rafael heard his cell phone ring, surged to his feet and snatched it off the side table. He checked the screen, saw his best friend's phone number and sighed in relief. "I must have called you a dozen times. What took you so long to hit me back?"

"Well, good morning to you, too," Stefano said with a chuckle. "What's up?"

"I need Paris's cell phone number."

"That's why you've been blowing up my phone?"

Rafael tucked his wallet into his front pocket. "Just give me the number. I'm pressed for time."

"What's the emergency?"

I had sex with Paris, and she skipped out on me in the middle of the night. I want an explanation and I want it now! Since Rafael couldn't tell his best friend the truth, not without raising suspicion, he lied. "I found her diamond necklace and I want to return it before she leaves for the States."

"You're too late. Her flight was at 7:00 a.m. She's long gone."

"Are you sure?"

"Yeah, she had breakfast with Cassandra before she left for the airport."

Rafael hung his head and dragged his hand down his face. He felt winded, as if he'd been kicked in the stomach.

"Just hang on to the necklace, and return it when Paris gets to Washington next Friday."

His ears perked up. "Paris is going to be in Washington?"

"She didn't tell you?"

No, but I'm sure there are a lot of other things she conveniently forgot to share.

"She has some important business matters to attend to at Excel Construction, and she's also speaking at the Women's Business Expo in March," Stefano continued.

Rafael's heartbeat quickened. "Are you sure?"

"Yeah, I got Cassandra tickets last week and she's superexcited about the event...."

An idea took shape in Rafael's mind as he listened to Stefano discuss the three-day conference at the W Hotel in Washington. Surprisingly, plotting his revenge, his sure-fire, get-even plan, gave him a natural high. He had to teach Paris a lesson, and knew just what to do to even the score.

"Thanks, man." Rafael shoved the necklace into his pocket and slipped on his leather dress shoes. "Have a great honeymoon. We'll talk soon."

Rafael snatched his tuxedo jacket off the chair and exited the suite. He heard someone shout his name and froze. Hanging his head, he released a deep, heavy sigh. *Damn.* Rafael glanced over his shoulder, spotted his brothers standing at the elevator. "Hey, guys, what's up?"

"I thought your suite was on the twentieth floor," Demetri said, leaning against the wall.

"It is."

"Then why are you sneaking out of Paris St. Clair's suite?"

"That's none of your damn business."

Nicco snapped his fingers. "I knew it. You ditched us last night to hook up with Paris, didn't you? That's why you ignored my calls and texts."

"I'll see you guys later. I have a meeting in Tuscany today, and I can't be late."

"Not so fast, Casanova. Your meeting isn't until three o'clock, so that gives you plenty of time to have breakfast with your brothers."

Rafael shook his head. "I have to pack."

"You brought a carry-on bag. Won't take you long."

The elevator doors slid open and his brothers pushed him inside.

"You have a lot of explaining to do, so we're heading down to the hotel restaurant."

"I can't go in there dressed like this," Rafael argued. "My clothes are a wrinkled mess."

"That's your fault. Next time you get your freak on remember to hang up your suit!"

"Shut up, Nicco."

Demetri wore a sympathetic smile. "Don't sweat it, bro. You look fine."

Then looks can be deceiving, he thought sadly. *I feel like crap.*

An hour later, Rafael, Nicco and Demetri were sitting at a corner booth inside the hotel restaurant eating breakfast. The dining room was occupied with a few sleepy-eyed diners, the air was filled with lip-smacking aromas and the pop song playing created a light, festive atmosphere. His brothers were having a great time, laughing and cracking jokes about their night out on the town, but Rafael couldn't get his mind off Paris. And every time he spotted a women with long black hair enter the restaurant his heartbeat sped up.

"So, how was your night of sex and debauchery?" Demetri cut a glance at Nicco and cleared his throat. "What happened between you and Paris?" he asked, draping an arm casually over the back of the booth. "And what's with all this secrecy?"

"What is this, twenty questions?"

"I'm serious, Rafael. You've been acting strange the past few weeks, and this situation with Paris St. Clair just proves how much you've changed."

I'm not the one who got engaged and became a love-struck fool, Demetri. You are!

Rafael picked up his mug and tasted his coffee. His brothers were watching his every move, and the air was thick with tension. Needing to clear his head, he told

Demetri and Nicco about his mind-blowing attraction to his first love. He deliberately skipped past the intimate details of his erotic encounter with Paris and instead spoke about all the fun they'd had together last night.

"Where is Paris now?"

Rafael shrugged and picked up his fork. "Your guess is as good as mine. I woke up this morning and she was gone."

"She left without saying goodbye?" Demetri gave his head a slow shake. "That's cold. No wonder you're pissed."

"I'm not pissed."

"Yes, you are. That's why your eyes are narrowed and your jaw is clenched. And if you gripped your water glass any tighter it would shatter into a million pieces."

Rafael took a deep breath, hoping it would calm his nerves, but it didn't. Every time he thought about Paris skipping out on him he wanted to punch a hole in the wall.

"I have to ask." Nicco leaned forward in his chair and stared Rafael dead in the eye. "Did you handle your business…in the bedroom?"

Rafael spoke through clenched teeth. "Just because I don't screw everything in a skirt doesn't mean I don't know how to please a woman."

Nicco held up his palms. "Bro, relax! I'm just playing devil's advocate."

"Spit it out. What are you trying to say?"

"Maybe it wasn't as good for her as it was for you—"

"Or maybe Paris left because she's scared," Demetri interjected.

"Of what?" Rafael asked, confused by his brother's words. "We're not strangers. We dated back in college, and we were extremely close."

"That was fifteen years ago." Demetri tossed a piece of cantaloupe into his mouth and chewed slowly. "Things are different now. Paris has changed, and so have you—"

"Thank God for that, because you used to be the biggest geek ever!"

"At least I wasn't a man-whore," Rafael retorted, glaring at Nicco.

"All right, guys, knock it off. We came here to talk, not to crack on each other."

Silence fell across the table. Rafael finished his omelet, washed it down with the rest of his coffee and wiped his mouth with his gold-rimmed napkin. Hearing his cell phone buzz, he took it out of his jacket pocket and punched in his password. He had dozens of new text messages, but found his mind wandering as he stared at the screen. He longed to hear Paris's voice, to see her, and wondered if she was thinking about him.

Doubt it, he thought glumly. *Why can't I meet an honest, trustworthy woman with family values and morals? And why can't she look, smell and sound like Paris St. Clair?*

"Gerald called me this morning," Nicco said.

Rafael glanced up from his cell phone. "He did? What did he say?"

"It looks like the arson investigation is finally heating up. No pun intended."

"Was he able to get a copy of Gracie's cell phone records?"

"Yeah, and he struck pay dirt." Nicco's eyes darkened a shade and held a menacing glare that spoke of his disgust. "The files prove Gracie and her brother, Trevor, were in Jariah's area at the time of the fire, and that's not all. Gracie was captured on video buying spray paint and bleach from a hardware store just days before Dolce Vita was trashed."

"So the police think she's good for the break-in at your restaurant, the shooting at the Beach Bentley Hotel and the arson attack at Jariah's condo complex?" Demetri asked.

"Can't say for sure. I'll know more once Gerald meets with detectives on Wednesday."

Rafael frowned and scratched his head. "You won't be at the meeting? But I thought you guys were heading back to Miami tonight?"

"We are, but Jariah and I have premarital counseling on Wednesdays, and—"

"Premarital counseling?" Rafael repeated. "But I thought you were the perfect couple! At least that's the impression you've always given me."

"We have a great relationship, but we don't always see eye to eye. No one does!"

"Are you thinking about postponing the wedding?" Demetri asked.

"Hell, no!" Nicco struck his fist on the table. "I'm marrying my baby and nothing's going to stop me."

Demetri and Rafael chuckled. Nicco was a cutup, always laughing and telling jokes, but when he spoke about Jariah and her daughter, his eyes brightened, his chest puffed up with pride and he became serious.

"Jariah's my soul mate, and I plan to be with her until the day I die. Thanks to couples therapy I've found even more things to love about her. I know deep in my heart that I wouldn't be the man I am today without her."

Intrigued, Rafael leaned forward. Normally, when his brothers started talking about their relationships, he zoned out, but today he wanted to hear what Nicco had to say. A year ago his bad-boy kid brother had had more groupies than any basketball team. Now he was crazy-in-love, engaged and so anxious to tie the knot it was all he could talk about.

"Relationships aren't easy, but I'm committed to making things work, and so is Jariah. We're in this thing together, and nothing can tear us apart."

Maybe I'm going about this situation with Paris all wrong, Rafael thought, stroking his jaw. *Maybe I should take a softer approach.*

"What are you going to do about Paris?" Nicco asked. He shrugged a shoulder.

"Don't leave us hanging, bro. Spill the beans."

"Why, so you can run back and tell your fiancées?" He gave a bitter laugh. "No way. Forget it. The fewer people who know about me and Paris the better."

"I thought you liked Angela." Demetri's voice was filled with hurt.

"I do. I think she's great, but I hate when you blab to her about my personal life."

Nicco scoffed. "What personal life? You don't have one. All you ever do is work!"

Stroking his own jaw, Demetri slanted his head as if deep in thought. "Who knows? Maybe now that he's reconnected with Paris that will change."

"You think?"

"Didn't you see them out on the dance floor last night?" Demetri wore a teasing smile and bumped Rafael's arm with his elbow. "You were gazing at her like a love-struck fool, and when Luigi told me you stole Paris away from him, I knew you had it bad."

"Luigi's a sleazeball," Rafael argued.

Nicco cocked a thick eyebrow. "And you're the perfect man for her, right?"

Yeah, bro, as a matter of fact I am.

"There's my handsome husband-to-be…." Angela excitedly yelled.

Rafael turned, saw Angela and Jariah approaching the booth and smiled. They were both strong, independent women who weren't afraid to speak their minds. He was proud of his brothers for snagging such incredible partners.

"Hola!" Jariah sat down beside Nicco and gave him a peck on the lips. "How is my baby doing this morning?"

"Great, now that you're here."

"Good answer!" she teased.

Everyone at the table laughed.

Rafael looked at his brothers, marveling at the admiration in their eyes. He recognized then what was missing from his own life: love. He wanted what Demetri and Nicco had. And secretly hoped to meet someone who'd love him unconditionally, a woman who didn't give a damn about his wealth and popularity. He'd been in love way back when in college, but he hadn't met anyone in the past fifteen years who stoked his fire the way Paris St. Clair did. She was in a league of her own, unlike anyone he'd ever met, and making love to her last night had only increased his desire for her, his insatiable hunger.

"I miss Ava, but this is turning out to be one hell of a weekend!" Jariah said with a laugh. "I can't remember the last time I had this much fun, and I owe it all to you, baby...."

Rafael took out his wallet, dropped two hundred euros on the table and got to his feet. It was time to go. His brothers and their girlfriends were kissing and hugging like teenagers out on a double date, and he felt like a third wheel. As always, the conversation would inevitably turn to wedding venues, flower arrangements and exotic honeymoon destinations. Rafael would rather go upstairs to his empty suite than listen to the couples discuss their upcoming summer nuptials.

"I'm going upstairs to pack," he said. "I'll see you guys later."

Jariah touched his forearm. "Don't go. We want to hear all about you and Paris."

Me and Paris? There's nothing to tell.

"Paris is an old friend and nothing more."

"Really?" Angela raised a thin, perfectly sculpted eyebrow. "You guys looked awfully cozy last night at the wedding reception...."

Rafael raised a finger in the air. "It was just a dance or two. It didn't mean anything."

"Are you sure? Because my instincts are telling me there's definitely a story here."

Demetri made his eyes big and wide. "Run, bro! She's on to you!"

Everyone at the table cracked up. The waiter arrived and loaded the empty plates and utensils on his silver trolley. Deciding to make a quick getaway, Rafael grabbed his cell phone and exited the hotel restaurant before Demetri's fiancée—a popular TV news reporter with a knack for uncovering the truth—could grill him about his one-night stand.

Chapter 10

Paris should have been on cloud nine. Her meeting with Ebony Garrett, the gregarious CEO of the multimillion-dollar franchise Discreet Boutiques, had gone extremely well. If everything went according to plan, Excel Construction would be building ten more stores next year. And that wasn't all. They had been voted most improved business by the Better Business Bureau.

When her father had called an hour after her meeting with the exciting news, her staff had danced around the conference room, cheering, shrieking and laughing, but all Paris could muster was a weak smile. Hours later, she still couldn't shake her melancholy mood.

Up to her neck in lavender-scented bubbles, she sat in her bathtub, sipping wine and listening to music. Jet lag was kicking her butt, and she had more aches and pains than a boxer. More tired than she could ever remember being, she rested her head against the rim and allowed the slow, sensuous love song to soothe her troubled mind. *What's the matter with me? Why do I feel so empty inside?*

Because you left Rafael without saying goodbye, her conscience reminded her.

Guilt tormented her. *He must think the worst of me.* At the time, leaving Rafael in her suite had seemed like a good idea. He was tired and sleeping so soundly in her bed. But when she arrived at the airport and saw all the lovey-dovey couples in the first-class lounge, Paris had felt like the scum of the earth. And when she arrived in Washington next Friday she planned to tell him just that.

If she could even muster the courage to face him

They'd had wild, passionate sex all night long. Just thinking about how she'd begged and moaned and screamed his name made her cheeks burn with embarrassment. Paris closed her eyes to stop the explicit images that flashed in her mind, but to no avail. All day long she'd thought of him and nothing else. She'd always had a weakness for tall, dark-haired guys, and her first love was still the sexiest piece of eye candy she'd ever seen.

And a sensuous lover.

His kisses, caresses and passion were unmatched, unlike anything she'd ever experienced. He'd explored her body, ravished every curve and slope, and just when Paris thought she'd had enough he'd given her more. They'd made love on the couch, in the shower and on the bed—three earth-shattering times—but Paris still couldn't believe it. If not for the hickeys on her neck and her sore thighs, she would have sworn she imagined the whole thing.

"Who is R.M., and why did he send you three-dozen roses?"

Startled, Paris shot up in the tub. Standing in the doorway, holding a glass vase filled with flowers, was her sister, Kennedy. Though the mother of three looked stylish in a belted sweater, leggings and ankle boots, Paris couldn't help but notice the dark circles under her eyes, and her lifeless brown skin.

"Are you trying to give me a heart attack?" Paris rested a hand on her chest and exhaled a deep breath. Her pulse pounded in her ears. "Don't sneak up on me like that. You scared me half to death."

"Sorry, sis. I was so anxious to see you I wasn't thinking."

Paris smiled for the first time all day. It didn't matter how stressful things were or how glum she felt, her sister always found a way to cheer her up. She was a petite powerhouse, and one of the strongest, most fearless women Paris knew. Kennedy had been her rock ever since their mother died, and she loved her sister more than anything in the world.

"Good thing I stopped by when I did or the delivery guy would have left with your pretty flowers." Kennedy closed her eyes and buried her nose in the oversize vase. "They smell divine. Where do you want me to put them?"

It was the largest flower arrangement Paris had ever seen. The colorful, long-stemmed roses flooded the room with their fragrant scent. "It doesn't matter. Anywhere is fine."

Kennedy set the vase down on the counter, plucked the card out of the plastic holder and read it out loud. "'We'll always have Venice, R.M.' What does that mean?" Her eyes tripled in size and she cupped a hand over her mouth. "OMG, you met someone at Cassandra's wedding, didn't you!"

"Scream louder. I don't think the family across the street heard you."

"Tell me who R.M. is or I'll unfriend you on Facebook."

Paris splashed water at her sister and cracked up when she shrieked like a kid on a roller coaster. She trusted Kennedy wholeheartedly, and knew she'd never betray her, but didn't feel comfortable talking about her one-night stand in Venice.

"I'm waiting," her sister trilled in a singsong voice.

Paris picked up her wineglass, and took a sip. "His name is Rafael Morretti."

"And," she pressed.

"And that's it. You wanted to know who R.M. was and I told you, so let it go."

Kennedy crossed her legs and propped a hand under her chin. "What's he like?"

He's smart, sweet, chivalrous and he has the sexiest eyes I've ever seen. "That depends on who you ask," she said vaguely, pretending to inspect her manicure.

"Wow, you're a real wealth of information."

Hoping her sister would move on to something else, Paris rolled her eyes to the ceiling.

"Why did he send you flowers?"

"Beats me."

"You're lying, and I'm going to find out why." Kennedy took her cell phone out of her pocket, slid her index finger across the screen and typed furiously. "Since you won't answer any of my questions, I'll just have to do some digging of my own."

"Fine."

Kennedy stuck out her tongue. "Bite me!"

Paris grabbed her towel off the hook, stepped out of the bathtub and swathed it around her body. "I'm going to get dressed," she said, picking up the flower arrangement as she exited the bathroom. "When you're finished playing detective, meet me downstairs."

Paris was in her kitchen, admiring the roses Rafael had sent her, when she heard Kennedy scream. High heels clacked on the hardwood floor, and the smell of hair spray tickled her nose.

"OMG! I think I'm in love!"

Holding up her cell phone, her sister marched over to the breakfast bar. All the blood in Paris's body shot straight to her core. A photograph of Rafael, dressed to kill in a sleek, charcoal-gray suit, was on the phone screen. Seeing his handsome face and how dreamy he looked made her panties instantly wet.

Paris dragged her gaze away from the cell phone, threw

open the pantry door and searched the shelves for something quick to make for dinner.

"This is Rafael Morretti?"

All she could do was nod. Her sister had the discerning nature of a private investigator. If Paris wanted to survive their conversation, she had to keep her mouth shut, her emotions in check and her horny body under control.

That's easier said than done, her conscience pointed out. *You're so weak for Rafael your body's still on fire from last night!*

"He's a hottie," Kennedy declared, leaning against the granite countertop. "And you can tell by his relaxed posture and smoldering gaze that he can work it between the sheets."

Girl, you have no idea.

"I bet he's hiding a gorgeous physique under that suit…."

Broad shoulders, a washboard stomach and eight delicious inches, but who's counting?

"Rafael Morretti deserves to be the Sexiest Man Alive!"

Kennedy licked her lips as if she were about to devour a plate of baby back ribs, and Paris couldn't resist poking fun at her. "Damn, girl, sometimes you're worse than a teenager! Have you forgotten that you're a Sunday school teacher and a PTA president?"

A smirk lit her almond-brown eyes. "I'm married, not dead! Besides, there's nothing wrong with looking."

"Does Anthony get a free pass to drool over beautiful women online, too?"

"Nope, and if I catch him, that's his ass!"

The sisters laughed and exchanged high fives.

"It says here that Rafael lives in Washington," Kennedy said, gesturing to her cell phone. "How did you guys meet?"

Paris thought for a moment, decided it couldn't hurt to

tell her sister the truth, and closed the pantry door. "Rafael and I dated when we were freshmen at University of Washington, and I ran into him at Cassandra and Stefano's wedding."

"No way!" Kennedy slanted her head as if deep in thought. "I don't remember you ever dating anyone named Rafael."

"You were too busy hanging out with your friends to care."

"Ouch. That's a low blow."

Feeling contrite, Paris linked arms with her sister. "We weren't close back then, and whenever I tried to talk to you about school or boys, you ignored me."

"I was pretty selfish back then, huh?"

"Still are," she quipped, laughing.

"On paper Rafael seems like a great catch, but is he a nice guy?"

"Kennedy, don't be silly. Nice guys don't exist."

"Of course they do, and if Rafael wasn't a good guy he wouldn't have sent you beautiful flowers." Kennedy squeezed her forearm, and spoke in a sympathetic tone. "You can't paint all men with the same brush just because you had one bad experience…."

Yeah, one bad experience that almost killed me.

"After Mom passed, I lost my reason for living, but then I met Anthony and fell head over heels in love." Kennedy's eyes twinkled and a dreamy expression came over her face. "And once I became a mother I realized there was no greater joy than having a child."

"Then why aren't you at home with your kids now?" Paris said with a laugh.

Her smile vanished. "I had to get out of there. Anthony's driving me crazy."

"Is everything okay?"

Kennedy sat down at the kitchen table and dropped her

face in her hands. Seconds passed before she spoke, and when she did her voice was grave. "Anthony lost his job."

"Oh, no, that's terrible. How's he holding up?"

"Not good. He's applied to tons of other computer software firms, but hasn't heard anything yet."

Paris rubbed her sister's back and told her not to worry. Listening to her talk about the strain in her marriage and the stress she was under at her public relations job, broke her heart. Paris wanted to do something to help, but what? The answer came to her in a flash. "Call Dad," she said. "He'll know what to do. He always does."

Kennedy shook her head so hard her honey-blond curls tumbled around her face. "No way. I talk to that man once every year during the holidays, and that's more than enough."

"Talk to him," Paris repeated. "He can give Anthony a job."

"No, thanks."

"Kennedy, you're being unreasonable. Think about your family, the kids—"

Her eyes narrowed and the corners of her mouth twitched. "I don't expect you to understand. You're the golden child. You have no idea how mean and insensitive Dad can be."

Paris dropped her hands to her sides. Her sister's icy tone put her on edge. Paris told herself to stay calm, but it was a struggle to keep her temper in check when all she wanted to do was scream. "The golden child? What's that supposed to mean?"

"You're his favorite. Always have been, always will be."

"No, I'm not. Dad loves us all the same."

"As if!" Kennedy gave a bitter laugh. "In Dad's eyes Oliver and I are screwups. You went to college, graduated with honors and became his right-hand man. Thanks to you, Excel Construction has grown by leaps and bounds the past ten years."

What the hell? How did our lighthearted conversation about love and relationships turn so ugly, so quick? Insulted, and confused by her sister's rant, Paris lashed back in self-defense. "Don't blame me for the mistakes you've made," she retorted. The anger in her voice ricocheted around the kitchen walls. "No one told you to get pregnant and drop out of college your sophomore year. That was your choice."

"At least I have a backbone and can think for myself."

Shocked by the verbal slap, Paris hitched a hand to her hip and glared at her sister.

"Unlike me," she continued, her voice filled with disgust, "you always do exactly what Dad says, and he rewards you handsomely for your obedience."

Paris wanted fight back, but shrugged off the criticism. "That's not true."

"Yes, it is. You quit cosmetology school because Dad said doing hair and makeup was beneath you. You drive a Lexus because that's the only car *he* likes, and when he tells you to jump you ask, 'How high?'"

"Mom's gone," Paris croaked, her throat suddenly dry and sore. "He's all we have left."

"No, he's all *you* have left. I have my husband and my children. I don't need Dad." Grumbling under her breath, Kennedy unzipped her leather handbag and took out a red heart-shaped envelope. "I didn't come over here to argue with you about Dad. I came to give you this."

"What is it?" Paris asked, taking the envelope from her sister's outstretched hand.

"Anthony and I are throwing an intimate soiree for our family and friends at The Hyatt to celebrate our anniversary." She beamed from ear to ear. "A lot of people didn't think we'd last six months let alone a strong sixteen years."

"Did you mail an invitation to Dad?"

"No, why would I? He's always been horrible to Anthony, and he shows zero interest in our kids. He sends a check every year for their birthdays, but it takes more than money and expensive gifts to be a good grandfather."

"Kennedy, don't be so hard on him. He's trying—"

"Trying, my ass."

Sick of arguing, Paris shook her head and exhaled a deep breath.

"Invite Rafael to be your date for the party," Kennedy said, her tone much warmer than before. "I'd love to meet him."

"I bet you would. You always did have a thing for Italian guys!" Laughing, Paris ripped open the envelope and read the invitation. Her heart fell and her shoulders sagged.

"What's wrong?"

"Kennedy, I'm so sorry, but I won't be able to come. The Excel Construction charity gala is the same day."

Her eyebrows merged together. "So? Skip it."

"I can't do that. Dad would disown me!"

"I survived." Kennedy eyed her coldly. "I don't make as much money as you do, and I'll probably never travel around the world or live in a million-dollar neighborhood, but I love my life and I wouldn't trade it for anything in the world. Can you say the same?"

An awkward silence fell between them.

Paris couldn't find her voice. Her sister's words replayed in her ears, taunting her like an invisible bully. *I love my life and I wouldn't trade it for anything in the world. Can you say the same?*

Sadness consumed her, causing memories of that tragic winter night to surface. Paris pressed her eyes shut and deleted every thought of her ex from her mind. She tried to think of something funny to say to lighten the mood, but came up empty.

"I better go." Kennedy swung her purse over her shoulder. "It's getting late, and Anthony and the kids are probably wondering where I am."

Paris snatched the cordless phone off the counter and gestured to the take-out menus taped to the stainless-steel fridge. "Don't go. I was just about to order in. We'll make mocktails, eat dinner and watch your favorite reality TV shows!"

"No, thanks. I've already overstayed my welcome as it is…."

"Don't say things like that. I love having you here. That's why I gave you a key."

"I'll give you a call later in the week."

Paris reached into her pocket, took out some folded bills and handed them to her sister. "Buy the kids pizza tonight, and take them shopping tomorrow."

"Keep it. Money's tight, but I'm not a pauper."

"I know. I just like spoiling the kids. That's what aunties do!" Paris hugged her sister and dropped the money inside her purse. "Are we okay? I hate when you're mad at me, and I didn't mean to upset you."

"I'm not mad, just disappointed, that's all."

"I'm happy for you and Anthony, and I wish I could come to your party. But I can't be in Atlanta and Washington at the same time."

Dropping her gaze to the floor, Kennedy twisted her gold wedding band around her finger. Her eyes were sad and her lips were trembling, but she spoke in a clear voice. "You just wait and see. Our anniversary bash is going to be the talk of the town! Everyone who loves and supports us will be there, and that's all that matters to me."

Wincing, Paris tried not to let her sadness show. Feeling guilty for the things she'd said earlier to Kennedy, she watched helplessly as her sister yanked open the front door and marched down the walkway.

Paris blinked back tears. She felt unhappier than she'd ever been and wished there was someone she could talk to. Thoughts of Rafael overwhelmed her mind, but she pushed them aside. She had no right to call him, not after the way she'd treated him in Venice.

Standing on the welcome mat, watching Kennedy drive away, Paris was hit with a startling truth: in less than twenty-four hours she'd screwed things up with her sister *and* the only man she'd ever truly loved.

Chapter 11

The moment the Boeing 747 landed at Dulles International Airport on Friday morning, Paris was off and running. She touched base with her assistant back in Atlanta, answered her emails and sent Kennedy a funny text message to lighten the mood between them.

By the time Paris reached the baggage claim area she'd checked off everything on her to-do list and revised her weekly schedule.

Tired and hungry, Paris stood in front of the carousel taping her foot impatiently on the floor. She'd been up since 5:00 a.m., and after weathering treacherous road conditions in Atlanta, had boarded an airplane filled with crabby travelers, wailing babies and bitchy flight attendants. Her stomach grumbled and groaned, but she ignored it. She'd eat when she reached the W Hotel Washington and not a moment sooner.

Paris touched her neck, remembering she'd lost her heart-shaped pendant, and sighed with regret. She'd called Hotel Excelsior every day since returning from Venice, hoping that a Good Samaritan had turned it in, but she had no such luck. Paris kept telling herself it didn't matter, that she could replace it with something more expensive from Cartier, but deep down she knew the piece was unique. Rafael had given her the necklace for her twentieth birthday, and she'd worn it every day for the past fifteen years. It had sentimental value and could never be

replaced. She'd always considered the necklace her good
luck charm and felt naked without it.

Shaking off her sadness, Paris raised her hunched shoulders and straightened her electric-blue blazer. She didn't
have time for a pity party. She had a speech to write for the
Women's Business Expo, contracts to read and a charity
gala to plan. Now more than ever she had to stay focused
and keep it together.

Swallowing a yawn, Paris pulled back the sleeve of
her blazer and checked the time on her wristwatch. If she
finished writing her speech by noon, she could squeeze
in a nap and a little retail therapy at her favorite Georgetown boutique.

"If you were a hamburger at McDonalds you'd be the
McGorgeous!"

Oh, brother, not again, Paris thought, groaning inwardly. *Why do lowlifes keep hitting on me? Do I have
the word* desperate *written across my forehead in yellow
neon marker?*

A guy dressed in a black bomber jacket and baggy
clothes saddled up beside her, wearing a toothy grin. Annoyed, she sucked her teeth and rolled her eyes to the ceiling. The stranger had tattoos, gold teeth, and gave off a
bad-boy vibe. He definitely wasn't her type. She preferred
athletic, clean-cut men with impeccable manners.

Men like Rafael Morretti.

Thoughts of the handsome Italian filled her mind. As
Paris reminisced about their time in Venice, she couldn't
help wondering if what Cassandra had told her was true.
Last night, while she was working in her home office, her
best friend had called to talk about her romantic Carib-
bean honeymoon. They'd chatted and laughed for hours,
but the moment Cassandra mentioned Rafael's name Paris

had lost her voice. Her tongue froze inside her mouth and her heart beat wildly.

"Rafael called Stefano in a panic the day you left Venice."

Paris played dumb. "Really? That's odd. I wonder why."

"I don't know. You tell me."

"There's nothing to tell."

"Oh, but I think there is. Rafael was supposed to go clubbing with the bridal party after the wedding, but he got on the elevator with you, and that's the last anyone saw of him."

"You make it sound like he was abducted!" Paris cracked up. "Maybe he changed his mind and crashed in his hotel suite."

"Or," Cassandra stressed, raising her voice, "maybe you put it on him, and he blacked out!"

Twenty-four hours later her friend's joke still made Paris laugh.

"Are you from around here or just visiting?"

Paris blinked and surfaced from her thoughts. Spotting her Versace suitcase on the luggage belt, she stepped past the five-foot nuisance running his mouth and grabbed her designer bag. Weaving through the crowd, she stalked through the airport, desperate to distance herself from the tattooed stranger with the weak-ass pickup lines.

Paris slid on her sunglasses, flung her pashmina scarf over her shoulders and strode confidently through the sliding glass doors. The sky looked gloomy but the air smelled clean and fresh. Taxicabs crawled along the glistening street, car horns blared in the distance and travelers rushed in and out of the busy airport doors.

The black Town Car idling at the curb flashed its headlights, and Paris hustled down the sidewalk as fast as her stiletto boots would allow. She threw open the back door, heaved her suitcase inside and buckled her seat belt. "W Hotel Washington, please."

The driver nodded and joined the slow-moving airport traffic.

Hearing her ring tone, Paris plopped her purse on her lap and rummaged around inside for her cell phone. Finding it, she clutched it in her hands. Her father's number popped up on the screen. Lowering her hands to her lap, Paris considered letting the call go to voice mail. Since returning from Venice, she'd spoken to her dad numerous times, and every time they spoke he was outright rude to her. Paris knew why he was calling, and didn't want to hear another word about the World of Concrete convention in Las Vegas next month.

The phone stopped ringing but started up again only seconds later.

"Good morning, Dad. How are you?" Paris asked, faking a cheery, upbeat voice.

"I don't have time for idle chitchat. Terrance Franklin should be here any minute now, and I don't want to keep him waiting."

"Oh, that's right, you're meeting to discuss his new inner-city project in Dallas."

His voice warmed. "I think building a community center in his grandfather's name is an excellent idea, and I want Excel Construction to be a part of the project."

"I agree." An idea sparked in her mind, and a smile curved her lips. "Dad, could you get Terrance Franklin's autograph for Anthony? He's a huge football fan, and Terrance is his all-time favorite player."

Her father made a disgusted sound. "I will do no such thing."

"Why not? It would mean the world to Anthony."

"I don't care. It's ill-mannered and highly inappropriate."

Confused, Paris stared down at her cell phone. "What is? I don't understand."

"Of course you don't. Your generation doesn't know the first thing about professionalism or social niceties," he complained. "Do you have any idea how foolish I'd look asking the Heisman Trophy winner for an autograph during our meeting?"

Paris strangled a groan. All that mattered to her father—besides making money and rubbing elbows with Washington's upper crust was being revered by his clients, associates and well-heeled friends at the Washington Golf and Country Club. He loved vintage wine, but never drank in public for fear of being labeled a drunk, dined only at five-star restaurants and flaunted his wealth in the hopes of ending up in the society pages.

"I didn't call to discuss proper business etiquette…."

His brisk tone cut into her thoughts.

"I called to give you the new password for the alarm. Get a pen and right it down."

"Dad, I'm not staying at the house."

"Why not? There's more than enough room for you at the mansion."

"I know, but I'll be coming and going for the next few weeks and I don't want to disturb you." Her excuse sounded pathetic but Paris didn't have the guts to tell him the truth. "Since the Women's Business Expo is being held at the convention center, I figured it made more sense to just book a suite at one of the nearby hotels."

Silence plagued the line. It lasted so long Paris feared her father had hung up.

"Hello? Dad? Are you still there?"

"Yes, of course. I'm just…thinking."

Paris heard papers shuffle and knew her dad was sitting behind his executive desk reading contracts and sipping Colombian coffee. He was a creature of habit who lived for rules and structure. And he wasn't happy unless he was calling the shots. That's why Paris chose to stay at a hotel and not at his lavish mansion.

"Do you have time to meet for dinner tonight or are you too busy?"

"Dad, don't be silly. I'm never too busy for you."

"You better say that! I'm the guy who signs your checks, and don't you forget it!"

His laugh startled her. Paris couldn't remember the last time she'd joked around with her dad, and hearing his loud chuckle warmed her heart. Their conversations were always about work, but tonight she planned to talk to her dad about Anthony and Kennedy's anniversary party, not ways to boost profits and productivity at Excel Construction.

"Good news," he said. "I pulled some strings and got you registered for the World of Concrete convention."

"Dad, I thought we talked about this. I'm not going."

"Of course you are. We go every year."

Yeah, and every year I consider faking my own death!

"This is not open for discussion, Paris. You're going and that's final."

"Why don't you take Oliver? He's never been to a World of Concrete convention."

Her father barked a laugh. "Don't be ridiculous. Your brother doesn't know the difference between a drill and a hammer! He'd be absolutely useless to me at the conference."

Paris bit her tongue, deciding not to argue with her dad. There was no way in hell she was going to the three-day conference in Las Vegas at the end of the month. And there was nothing he could say or do to change her mind.

Maybe he'll fire me! she thought hopefully. *Then I could open the beauty salon of my dreams.*

"I have to go," he said briskly. "Be at Bourbon Steak by seven o'clock sharp."

Taking a deep breath, Paris disconnected the call and stretched her legs out. Thankfully, the driver didn't try to make conversation, and as she closed her eyes and sank into her seat, she decided she'd reward him nicely for his silence. Alone with her thoughts, she allowed the stress and anxiety of the past seventy-two hours to fade away.

Thoughts of Rafael inundated her mind again, and for some unexplainable reason she wondered what life would be like if he was her man. Would he accompany her to black-tie events? Would he make an effort to get along with her boisterous, dysfunctional family? And most important, would he be open and honest and love her unconditionally?

Paris shook her head and chided herself for being silly. Back when they were dating, Rafael used to love to take her out, but now he was a homebody who'd rather read the *Wall Street Journal* than party at the hottest nightclubs, and that would never change. He preferred spending quiet evenings at home, while she enjoyed red-carpet events, movie premiers and lively concerts. *We're more different than alike, so why am I fantasizing about him? And why do I wish he was here with me right now?*

Her head jumped from one thought to the next. Paris treasured her independence, and didn't want love to cramp her style. But she couldn't deny her feelings for Rafael. She wanted him, and not just because he had juicy lips and the body of a Greek god. He was a romantic at heart, chivalrous and kind, and she loved being with him.

Memories of New Year's Eve consumed her. It had been the most sensuous night of her life, and reminiscing about her epic encounter with Rafael triggered a rush of de-

sire. Her feelings for him were so powerful and intense
they scared her. He knew just what to say to make her
smile, never failed to tell her she was smart and beautiful
and made love to her with reckless abandon. His kiss was
magic, his touch explosive, and a week after their one-night
stand, Paris was *still* tingling between her legs.

Haunted by his smile, she struggled to control her emotions. Their behavior on New Year's Eve was hard to jus-
tify, and impossible to condone, so why was she reliving
every moment of that night? And why was she itching to
make love to him again?

Paris longed to hear his voice, could almost feel his
soft, tender caress. Tapping her index finger on her cell
phone, she wrestled over what to do about him. *Should I
or shouldn't I?* she wondered, trying to ignore the suffocating knot in the pit of her stomach.

The town car slowed and then stopped. Paris opened her
eyes and looked out the window. She saw children playing
in the snow, mothers trudging up the block pushing baby
strollers and mail carriers jogging from one brownstone
to the next. Before she could ask the driver if he was lost,
he got out of the car and slammed the door.

I hope he isn't doing personal errands on my dime, or—

A gush of cold air flooded the car when the back door
swung open. Her teeth chattered and she shivered, but
when she looked up as the driver took her hand to help her
out of the car, a delicious heat spread through her body.

Paris couldn't believe her eyes. The town car driver was
Rafael. The man she'd made sweet love to seven days earlier. Panic rose in her chest and fear coated her throat. Her
first impulse was to try to make a break for it, but Paris
knew she wouldn't get far.

She touched a hand to her chest. Her heart slammed
into her rib cage, stealing her breath and her voice. If she

didn't get her emotions under control she was going to have a panic attack, right there on the street.

Breathing deeply slowed down her erratic heartbeat. Paris tried to speak, wanting desperately to apologize for the way she'd treated him in Venice, but couldn't get the words out.

"Good morning, angel eyes. You're looking gorgeous, as usual."

The sound of his dreamy, sensuous voice caused desire to well up inside her. Paris felt the urge to touch him, and an even stronger urge to kiss him all over. Unexpectedly seeing Rafael again made her feel excited and nervous at the same time. But all she could think about was how handsome he looked in his crisp black uniform.

What the hell was going on? Rafael wasn't a chauffeur, so why was he dressed like one? Nothing made sense, but Paris still didn't have the presence of mind to speak. Not when he was staring intently at her, wearing a boyish grin. He smelled of expensive cologne, looked devilishly handsome, and when he reached out and caressed her cheek, her thoughts took an erotic detour. "Thanks for the flowers," she blurted out. "They're beautiful, and the card was sweet."

"I'm glad you liked them. I remembered how much you love roses and thought they'd make a nice thank-you gift."

Confused, Paris frowned. "A thank-you gift? But I didn't do anything."

"Oh, but you did." His gaze smoldered with longing. "I flew to New York yesterday to see my parents, and when I gave my mom the gifts you helped me pick out for her she squealed like an adolescent girl!"

Paris laughed. "Of course she did. *Everyone* loves Chanel!"

"Why did you leave Venice without saying goodbye?"

He wants to talk about this here, now, in the middle of the sidewalk? Overwhelmed with guilt, and fear of being put on the spot, Paris blurted out the only thing she could think of in the moment. "I had an early morning flight and I didn't want to…um, wake you." Her voice faltered and her tongue tripped over the lie. Paris wasn't afraid of anything and usually said exactly what was on her mind. But the thought of telling Rafael the truth—that she'd skipped town because she was embarrassed about her raunchy behavior in bed and was too ashamed to face him—made her break out in hives.

"I'm sorry. I wasn't thinking. I should have said goodbye, but I was in a rush."

Rafael took off his cap and tucked it under his arm. "Are you sure that's all it was?"

"Come again?" She stared up at him, meeting his dark gaze head-on. "I don't understand what you're asking."

"Did I please you in bed?"

Paris inhaled sharply. *Are you for real? Isn't it obvious?* Thinking about their New Year's Eve escapade made her yearn for more. More kissing, more caressing, more explosive sex in unlikely places. Paris wanted Rafael so badly it hurt, but she restrained herself from touching him. Because if she did, there was no telling where things would end up, and Paris wanted to avoid getting arrested in her hometown for indecent exposure.

"I thought maybe you left because I was bad in bed and you didn't want to face me."

His confession blew her away, making her feel worse than she already did. Paris heard the vulnerability in his voice, the sadness, and knew she had to put his fears to rest. "That's absurd, and you know it." Losing the war with her flesh, she placed a hand on his chest and gave him a peck on the cheek. "You're an amazing lover, Rafael, and I wouldn't trade our night together for anything in the world."

A half smile crossed his mouth. "I'm glad we cleared the air."

Paris giggled and shook her head in disbelief.

"What's so funny?"

"This is crazy. I can't believe you're here. I was just thinking about calling you."

His hands moved down her arms and around her waist. "Thank God you didn't because if my cell had gone off inside the car that would've ruined the surprise."

"Yes, and what a surprise it was," she quipped. "I almost fainted when I saw you!"

Rafael chuckled long and hard, and Paris knew all was forgiven.

"It's chilly out here. Let's head inside." Rafael activated the car alarm and drew her to his side. "I hope you're starving, because I made all your favorites for breakfast."

"Where are we going? You live around here?"

He smiled, gesturing at the large Colonial-style house to their left, and patted her hip affectionately. "I've planned a fun-filled day for you, Ms. St. Clair, and a few more big surprises."

"If I don't check into the hotel by noon I'll lose my suite."

"Then you can stay here with me," he said in a smooth voice.

"Rafael, I can't. That's insane."

"Not to me. I love the idea of taking care of you."

Paris felt her heart melt, and knew she had stars in her eyes. At a loss over what to do, she weighed her options. She could call a cab to take her to the hotel, or have a long, luxurious brunch with Rafael. The answer should have been a no-brainer, but Paris couldn't shake her fear of being alone with him again.

"After we have breakfast I'll take you straight to the W Hotel."

His gaze held her in its powerful grip, reduced her to a quivering mess in a Christian Dior pantsuit. And when Rafael leaned in, laying a slow, lingering kiss on her lips, Paris knew she didn't have a chance in hell of resisting him.

Chapter 12

"Are you ready for dessert?"

Paris put her fork down on her plate, sank back into the padded chair and wiped her mouth with her napkin. Rafael had made all her favorites—chocolate croissants, strawberry-stuffed French toast, ham and cheese frittatas—and because of his persuasive charms she'd had second helpings and one Irish coffee too many. She was enjoying his company, the old-school songs playing in the background and all the scrumptious food, but she couldn't eat another bite. "No, thanks. Nothing for me."

Rafael cocked an eyebrow. "Are you sure?"

"Positive."

"There must be something I can do to change your mind...."

Crossing her legs, she played with her scarf. Her heart beat with a mixture of excitement and apprehension. Her throat was so dry it hurt to swallow. They'd been laughing and flirting since they sat down to eat and Paris was having a great time. Rafael made her feel like the only woman in the world, and every time he flashed his pearly whites at her she felt light-headed and giddy.

"You love dessert," he teased. "Don't try to deny it. I've seen you in action."

"Guilty as charged. I'm a chocolate addict and proud of it!" she said with a laugh. "I overindulged in Venice, and if

I want to fit into the gorgeous Christian Dior suit I bought for the Women's Business Expo, I have to quit pigging out."

"A few sweets won't hurt. You have a gorgeous body, and that will never change."

"What's on the menu?" Paris asked, wetting her lips with her tongue.

"You'll just have to wait and see."

She pursed her lips and faked a scowl. "You are *such* a tease."

"Close your eyes."

"Why? What do you have up your sleeve now?"

Rafael broke into a slow, sexy grin. "There's only one way to find out...."

Curious, she did as she was told. Paris didn't hear Rafael walk around the dining room table, but she sensed him beside her and knew he was just inches away from her face. Her pulse rate shot up. Rafael's hands explored her flesh, moved slowly down her neck, over her shoulders and along her arms. His touch made her wet, filled her with longing and desire. Her heart clapped like thunder, and the sound of her fast, heavy breathing drowned out the soulful, sensuous music playing on the stereo.

Paris felt something brush against her collarbone and opened her eyes. "My necklace!" she shrieked, clutching the heart-shaped pendant to her chest. "I thought I'd lost it forever. Where did you find it?"

"Under the bed in your hotel suite."

A sigh of relief fell from her lips as she admired her necklace. "Oh, thank God. I've been beating myself up all week for losing it."

"I'm surprised you still wear it." Rafael leaned against the table. "I figured you tossed it in the trash after we broke up."

"No, never, it's a gorgeous piece of jewelry and one of my most cherished possessions."

He looked pleased, and when he asked about his "finder's fee," Paris cracked up. "Don't worry," she said, standing up. "I have it right here."

"Now, that's what I'm talking about!"

Paris cupped his face in her hands and kissed the corner of his mouth. "Thanks for returning my necklace, Rafael. You're a lifesaver."

"And you're beautiful."

The predatory gleam in his eyes made her mouth dry and her sex tingle, but Paris knew better than to act on her desires. What happened in Venice was a onetime thing, something on the spur of the moment after too many glasses of champagne. Today she was sober, completely in control and determined to keep her wits about her. "I'll help you clear the table before I go," she said, stacking the utensils on the empty plates. "It's almost three o'clock, and I have a million things to do before this evening."

"You're not going anywhere."

The twinkle in his eyes and the grin on his lips belied his curt tone.

"Is that so?"

"Yes, it is."

Paris hid a smile. His voice was firm, as if the matter was nonnegotiable, and his posture was one of confidence and self-assurance. She had to admit, his take-charge demeanor was damn sexy. It made her hot, way down below, and his fiery gaze was a turn-on.

"You belong to me for the rest of the weekend."

"That's not going to go over well with my dad," she said with a laugh. "We're meeting at Bourbon Steak for dinner, and if I'm a no-show there'll be hell to pay."

"Do you always do everything your father says?"

"I like to keep the peace."

"Is that why you're going to the World of Concrete convention next month?"

Smirking, Paris swiped a napkin off the table and chucked it at him. "You were supposed to be driving, mister, not eavesdropping on my conversation."

"You don't need anyone to run your life, Paris. You're smart enough to make your own decisions. Always have been."

Deep in thought, she fiddled with her bracelet, running her fingers slowly over each delicate pearl. "After my mother died, I was lost and inconsolable, and if not for my father I would have gone down the wrong path like my brother and sister. He made a lot of sacrifices for me, and I feel like I owe all my success to him."

"I understand that. My parents worked hard to provide a good life for me and my brothers after we immigrated to the U.S. But although I love them dearly, I won't let them run my life." He added, with a wry smile, "And believe me they've tried, especially my mother!"

Paris gave serious thought to what he'd said. She was tired of her dad yelling at her and ordering her around, but she didn't have it in her to stand up to him. She desired her father's approval more than anything, often felt incomplete without it. And as Paris cleaned the dining room she realized that would probably never change.

"Oh, no, you don't." Rafael gripped her shoulders and steered her out of the room. "Go into the living room and relax."

"Are you sure? I don't mind helping."

"I'm positive," he said with a fervent nod of his head. "After I clean the kitchen, I'll prepare dessert then feed the dogs. It won't take long, I promise."

"I feel terrible that you put them outside. My allergies aren't that bad."

"Don't be. You're much better company, and you smell nicer, too."

Tickled pink, Paris concealed the girlish smile threatening to explode onto her face.

"Mi casa es su casa." Rafael lowered his head and dropped a kiss on her cheek. "Make yourself at home. I won't be long."

He picked up the stack of dirty dishes and set off for the kitchen.

I swear his lips are going to be the death of me! Paris left the dining room feeling jovial. The paintings along the cream-colored walls depicted rolling hills, clear blue skies and the pictures of Rafael and his beloved dogs made her heart soften like a marshmallow. Thinking about her charming host and all the laughs they'd shared that afternoon brought a smile to her face. No one had ever made her a home-cooked meal or gone to such extraordinary lengths to impress her. Paris was deeply touched by his thoughtfulness.

In the living room, wall lamps emitted a soft glow, potted candles perfumed the air with a lavender fragrance and arched picture windows offered breathtaking views of the city. Outside, the breeze whistled through the trees, and thick white snowflakes fell from the sky.

Paris put her cell phone on the table, sat down on the leather couch and tucked her feet underneath her. She loved the swank decor in Rafael's bachelor pad and admired the eye-catching sculptures and vibrant artwork. The black-and-white color scheme, vaulted ceilings and plush, chocolate-brown furniture made the two-story house cozy and inviting. And as Paris grooved to the D'Angelo song playing on the stereo, she felt relaxed and at ease.

Suddenly the scent of cinnamon filled the air. Hearing footsteps behind her, Paris glanced over her shoulder. Her pulse galloped like a Thoroughbred at the Kentucky Derby. Rafael stalked into the living room wearing his signature dreamy smile, and her heart overflowed with gratitude.

He knew how to treat a woman right, and for as long as Paris lived she'd never forget how special he'd made her feel every time they were together.

He walked with purpose, moved with such confidence and swagger it was impossible for her not to drool like one of his dogs. He was holding a silver tray, and when he set it on the coffee table Paris couldn't decide what to do first: devour him or the desserts.

Determined to remain under control, Paris tore her gaze away from him and buried her hands in her lap.

"I made these just for you." Rafael sat down beside her on the couch and picked up the plate of cookies. "Go on, help yourself."

Paris did. The fried, doughnut-like cookies were soft, warm, and so damn good she ate four. "What?" she asked sheepishly, helping herself to another one. "You said to eat up."

"And I meant it. There are lots more in the kitchen."

Paris dunked her cookie in her Irish coffee and took a small bite. Chewing slowly, she savored the warm, sweet treat. "I can't believe you bake."

"Why? Because I'm a guy?"

"Uh, yeah!" She laughed. "You don't strike me as the baking type, but I'm glad you are because these cookies are out of this world. You've got skills, man!"

"That means a lot, coming from you."

He spoke in a low, husky voice, one Paris found undeniably sexy. She couldn't take her eyes off of him, couldn't look away for a second, and wished his hands were stroking her body.

"Well, just so you know, there's a lot more to me than meets the eye."

"Oh?" Paris raised an eyebrow. "Enlighten me. I'm all ears."

His grin was sly and mischievous. "What do you want to know?"

He gave her a long, meaningful look. Paris felt vulnerable, exposed, as if she was sitting on the couch buck naked. It was hard to think when Rafael was staring intently at her, but she asked the question at the forefront of her mind. "Why did your last relationship end?"

His smile fell away and the muscles in his jaw tightened. "I'm surprised you don't know. The story was all over the news for weeks."

Intrigued, Paris turned toward him, giving him her undivided attention.

"My ex-girlfriend gave a tell-all interview about me and my family to *Celebrity Scoop*."

"That's terrible," Paris said, disgusted. "You should have sued her ass for defamation."

"I considered it, but once the magazine hit stores I changed my mind. Fighting Cicely in court seemed like a waste of time and money. I was too busy overseeing the development of our New York office to be bothered." Rafael cleared his throat and rubbed a hand across the back of his neck. "My dad was pissed because she told the magazine our family has ties to the Mafia, but her allegations didn't faze me. Cicely Cohen isn't the first person to try and capitalize off my last name, and she probably won't be the last."

Curiosity pushed Paris to ask, "Did you love her?"

"No, and when I had dinner with my brothers and their girlfriends, I realized how pathetic my relationship with Cicely was. There was no passion, no fire, and after I caught her in numerous lies I decided to call it quits. We broke up nine months ago, and I haven't spoke to her since."

His eyes probed her face, and her flesh caught fire.

"I've never loved anyone the way I love you, and I doubt I ever will."

Paris shifted uncomfortably in her chair and fiddled with her diamond ring on her left hand. "It sounds like you're better off without her," she said, wishing her voice didn't sound so squeaky. "What she did to you was cold and calculated."

"It was, but I survived, and the ordeal brought me and my family closer together."

Paris could relate to what he was saying and nodded in understanding. "It's hard to find people to trust. Everyone's hungry for fame and fortune, and will do just about anything to get both." Memories of the past made her heart throb with pain, but she pushed her thoughts aside. "I've been betrayed, too, but all those painful experiences made me a better judge of character and a stronger, more independent woman."

"It's you against the world, right?"

"Yeah, it is, and that's just the way I like it."

"I know how you feel. I have my family and that's all I need." Rafael picked up his mug and tasted his coffee. "I have the worst luck with women, and if my parents weren't pressuring me to get hitched I'd probably be a lifelong bachelor like George Clooney."

"Your mom is desperate for grandbabies, huh?"

Rafael groaned as if in physical pain. "Desperate is an understatement. Her new hobby is hooking me up on blind dates with her friends' daughters and introducing me to random women on the street."

"You poor thing. It must be *such* a drag meeting beautiful women 24/7."

"Thank you!" Rafael pumped his fist in the air as if he was cheering on his favorite basketball team. "Finally! Someone who understands my plight!"

Paris smirked.

A spirited conversation about love and relationships ensued, and when Rafael told her about his blind date from hell, Paris burst out laughing. Laughing so long and hard, tears gushed down her cheeks. For the first time in months, she felt happy. She couldn't stop smiling, didn't try to hide her feelings. Rafael was kind-hearted, romantic and chivalrous, and she was having a blast with him.

"You couldn't pay me to attend another holiday jam," he said, resting a hand comfortably on his knee. He looked as relaxed as a sun-seeker stretched out on Champagne Beach, and spoke freely, without restraint. "Singles events just aren't for me. I'd rather work or play poker with the guys than stand around making conversation with a bunch of people I have absolutely no interest in."

His words threw her, making her wonder what had happened to the friendly, outgoing guy she'd fallen hard for her freshman year of college. "When did you become so antisocial? When we in college you used to love going out and meeting new people."

"Things were a lot easier back in school. No one at U of W knew my family had money, so my father's wealth was never an issue. But these days I can't go anywhere without someone trying to cash in on the Morretti name."

"I hear you. I'm so tired of being lied to and disappointed that I refuse to date."

"Tell me about your last serious relationship."

The statement and the intensity of Rafael's gaze caught her off guard. Paris drew a deep breath, but her pulse was drumming so loudly in her ears she couldn't think straight. It hurt to think about her ex-boyfriend and the thought of confiding in Rafael about her past made her burn with shame.

Needing a moment to collect her thoughts, she stood and wandered over to the window beside the towering bookshelf. The streets were deserted, blanketed with snow, and hundreds of stars lit up the night sky. "This is a nice neighborhood. I love how quiet and peaceful it is. Have you lived here a long time?"

"You're trying to change the subject."

Paris struggled for a suitable response but came up empty. She heard footsteps cross the hardwood floor, saw his refection in the window and felt her body tense. Rafael stopped behind her, just inches away. Suddenly it became hard to breathe, difficult to swallow, and she couldn't think of a single thing to say.

Perspiration drenched her body, made her palms slick with sweat. The walls were closing in on her, the tension in the room so suffocating she felt as if she was trapped in an elevator with a hundred other people. Her throat closed up and her tongue lay limp in her mouth. Paris didn't want to talk to Rafael about her ex; she just couldn't do it, not today, and likely never. She made up her mind to call a cab as soon as her hands quit shaking.

"I just want to get to know you again. Is that so bad?"

Rafael touched her shoulder, and she reluctantly turned to face him. Bad idea. Seeing the compassion and concern on his handsome face made her eyes sting. A flood of tears momentarily blinded her, causing the living room to swim out of focus.

"Angel eyes, I'm sorry. I didn't mean to make you cry."

Embarrassed for letting her emotions get the best of her, she shook her head and waved her hands in front of her face. "Don't be silly. I'm not crying. It's just my allergies acting up again...."

He closed his arms around her, engulfing her cold, trembling body in a hug. Paris stood perfectly still. She tried not to notice how good it felt being in his arms. As he stroked her hair, her fears abated. Her tears dried up, her vision cleared and her hands quit shaking. The music, his soothing touch and the promises he whispered in her ears were her undoing. Desire overtook her like a crook lying in wait. Paris tried damn hard not to cross the line, promised herself she wouldn't throw herself at him again, but her body betrayed her.

Her mouth boldly claimed his lips, and her hands stroked his chest. He tasted sweet, like chocolate, and the rich, intoxicating flavor turned her on. She wanted more, needed more, and had plans to get it, too. The kiss roused her passion, filled her with an insatiable, mind-blowing hunger. His tongue made love to her mouth. Rafael was saying and doing all the things she liked, and Paris loved every sensuous minute of it.

Kissing passionately, they stroked and caressed each other like two people desperately in love. Paris lost all reason, and all sense of time and place. When her cell phone rang, she blocked out the intrusive noise. She was with Rafael, a man she'd loved and adored since she was nineteen years old, and she didn't want anything to ruin their time together.

She slid a hand under Rafael's shirt, but froze when he broke off the kiss. "What's the matter?" she asked, tenderly caressing his face. Paris loved touching him, liked stroking the hard contours of his cheekbones and jaw. Admiring his thick eyelashes and creamy brown skin, she marveled at what a handsome man he'd become over the years.

"I can't do this. It wouldn't be right." Rafael shook his head and dropped his hands to his sides. He looked troubled, as if his mind and body were at odds, and he avoided meeting her gaze. "I want you more than I've ever wanted anyone, but I can't sleep with you."

"Come again?" she blurted out, convinced she'd misheard him.

"I promised myself I'd keep my hands off you this weekend, and I'll feel defeated if I go back on my word."

Paris was confused by his mind-blowing confession,

but she didn't let her true feelings show. "Good thing I packed my vibrator in my suitcase, or I'd be *really* disappointed right now." She had spoken those words to lighten the mood, and earned a hearty chuckle from Rafael. He drew her back into the comfort of his arms and kissed her forehead. "I want more than one night with you, Paris. I love being with you and I want us to be exclusive."

"Five minutes ago you said you wanted to be a lifelong bachelor."

"If I can't have you, I don't want anyone."

Paris shook off his words, not daring to believe that they were true. "I live in Atlanta."

"We discussed this already, remember? That's not a deal breaker."

"Long-distance relationships never work."

"Are you always this optimistic?" Rafael cupped her chin and wore a stern, no-nonsense expression. "You can trust me with your heart, Paris. I won't hurt you, and you'll never have to worry about me betraying you. I'm fiercely loyal and dedicated to the people I love."

Realization dawned, and Paris felt her eyes widen and tear up. *Holy heavens! He's serious.*

"I don't know if I'm ready to be in another relationship," she murmured.

"We'll take things slow. As slow as you want. I want something real with you, something lasting, and I don't want our relationship clouded by lust," he told her. "I think we should hold off on making love for the time being."

"Where was all that self-control and level-headed thinking in Venice?"

"I couldn't help myself." Rafael brushed his nose against hers, and she laughed. "You looked so beautiful on New Year's Eve I fell hopelessly under your spell."

"And tonight?"

"I'm going to be a perfect gentleman."

"Don't be. I like when you're mischievous in bed."

His eyes darkened a shade and his grip tightened around her waist. "I'm warning you," he growled, his words a deep, sexy command. "Don't start something you can't finish."

Wearing a coy smirk, Paris seized his hands and slid them under her blouse. Excitement danced inside her, warmed and pricked her flesh as their bodies came together. She used his fingers to massage her breasts, to cup and knead her erect nipples, and then moaned in his ear, "I want to make you come with my mouth...."

The devilish gleam that lit his eyes said it all.

"Damn it to hell!" Rafael scooped Paris up, tossed her over his shoulder and playfully smacked her on the ass. She shrieked in laughter as he did it again, then jogged up the stairs.

Chapter 13

"This is for the game. The next point wins the match," Rafael announced, bouncing the tennis ball on the indoor court at the Washington Golf and Country Club. "I'm going to enjoy bragging about my come-from-behind win, especially after all the gloating you did yesterday when you beat me at Scrabble."

Narrowing her eyes with determination, Paris gripped her tennis racket and rocked eagerly from side to side. "Bring it on, pretty boy. Let's do this!"

As the ball left Rafael's hand, Paris knew it was going to be a soft serve down the middle and raced toward the net like a bat out of hell. The ball sailed in the air, and she hit it with an explosive forehand. It whizzed past Rafael, clipped the solid white line and hit the back of the wall. "Yahoo! I won!" Raising her hands in victory, she danced around the court. "You owe me a home-cooked meal, *and* a foot massage!"

"You cheated," Rafael said, wiping his forehead with a blue face towel.

"No, I didn't. I won fair and square, and you know it."

Rafael stepped over the net and swept Paris up in his arms. "How do you expect me to concentrate on my game when you're running around the court in this sexy, pink dress?"

"But you bought it for me!" she argued, playfully swatting his shoulder.

"I did, didn't I?"

His teasing smile made her laugh. Since arriving in Washington two weeks earlier they'd explored Chinatown, the open-air markets and the designer stores in Union Station. In his favorite used book store, they sat in comfy arm chairs, reading eighteenth-century poetry and feeding each other chocolate. On weekends, they hiked Great Falls Park, strolled hand-in-hand through Georgetown and cooked in his gourmet kitchen. Yesterday, after shopping at Mazza Gallerie, they'd returned to his brownstone and spent the rest of the night in each other's arms. They had great talks about their hopes and dreams and Paris wasn't afraid to open up to him about her fear and insecurities.

"Are you going to model the lingerie I bought you at Discreet Boutiques?" he asked, stroking her hips. "I'm dying to see you in that French maid costume."

"Only if you're a *very* good boy."

"Then I'll be on my best behavior for the rest of the day."

Rafael grabbed her butt, and Paris giggled. He was putting on a show, deliberately trying to make her laugh, and it worked. He made her forget everything—the pain of her past, her insecurities, her strained relationship with her father—and when he cupped her chin and kissed her tenderly on the lips, she felt more desirable than ever.

"We better stop before they kick us out," he joked, clasping her hand. Rafael looked dreamy in his white polo shirt and shorts, and as they exited the tennis court Paris noticed country club members—some old enough to be his mother—checking him out. To make it clear he was taken, she snuggled against him. "Do you still want to go to the Smithsonian today?"

Rafael nodded. "Yes, and after our private tour I'm taking you to my favorite Greek restaurant for lunch. Sound good?"

I don't care where we go or what we do as long as we're together. Paris felt safe, at home in his arms, and marvelled at how close they'd become since he'd "kidnapped her" two weeks earlier. The past fifteen years hadn't changed anything; Rafael was still the only man she wanted, the only man who knew her inside and out. He found unique, unexpected ways to make her feel special, and Paris loved him for it. More than she'd ever loved anyone. *Is this our chance to finally get it right? Can we have the relationship I've always dreamed of?*

They strode through the country club, hand-in-hand, and stopped in front of the fitness center to speak to one of Rafael's golf buddies. Paris was surprised when he introduced her as his girlfriend, but smiled politely at the cardiologist and made small talk. When the conversation turned to business, Paris gazed out the window and admired the breathtaking view of the Potomac River. Once known as the "Playground of Presidents," the Washington Golf and Country Club was one of the most exclusive clubs in the state. Built on 120 acres of lush, green grass, the property had everything a rich man could want: an 18-hole golf course, a heated swimming pool, a tap room and a five-star restaurant. The antique furnishings, ivory walls and muted color scheme evoked feelings of calm. Members spoke in refined voices, children were seen, not heard, and the faint scent of cigar smoke wafted through the air.

"Are you bringing this lovely lady with you to the Kennedy Center Spring Gala?"

"Of course," Rafael said proudly, kissing her forehead. "We lost touch after graduation, but now that we've reunited I'm not letting her out of my sight!"

The cardiologist left, and they continued through the main floor. Paris glanced into the cocktail lounge, but was careful not to make eye contact with anyone. She wasn't ready to tell her dad she was dating and hoped they didn't run into any of her father's friends or business associates. Curious about something Rafael had said earlier, she turned to him and asked, "Why did you introduce me to Austin as your girlfriend?"

"Because you are."

"But I've only been back in town for a couple weeks."

Rafael stopped at the entrance of the library and pulled her inside the empty, sun-drenched room. "We need to talk privately, and I don't want anyone to interrupt us," he said, resting his hand comfortably on her waist.

Amused, she hid a smirk. "Go on, Mr. Morretti. You have my undivided attention."

Rafael took her hand, kissed it and placed it flat against his chest. "At this point in my life I'm looking for a woman with my heart, not my eyes, and its leading me straight to you."

Moved by the sincerity of his words, she draped her arms around his neck and gave him a deep, sensuous kiss. Her heart overflowed with love and admiration as they feasted on each other's mouths. His touch was magic, and his caress roused her hunger.

"I can't get enough of you, Paris. I want you every second of every day, and I'm not ashamed to admit it," he whispered, nibbling at the corner of her lips. "It's time to get you home and *out* of this dress."

"Why wait?" Paris flashed a cheeky smile. "Let's make love in your BMW!"

"We could get arrested."

"That's a risk I'm willing to take."

Rafael cocked an eyebrow. "Don't start nothing won't be nothing."

"I'm starting it, right here, right now." Stroking his forearms and rock-hard chest excited her, and suddenly all Paris could think about was making love to Rafael. She saw his eyes widen, sensed his growing desire and knew she had him right where she wanted him. "I have to make sure you don't forget me when I return to Atlanta—"

"You're not the kind of woman a man forgets."

"Not even a man who has young beauties throwing themselves at him every day?"

"Paris, you are and always will be the only woman I want."

His cell phone rang, and he wore a contrite expression. "This will only take a minute." Rafael took his iPhone out of his back pocket, checked the number on the screen and put it to his ear. He was only on the phone for a few seconds, but when he ended the call his face was a dark, angry mask. "That was Elite Security. The alarm went off again."

"That's the second time this week."

Rafael shrugged a shoulder. "It's a pain in the ass, but I have to go check it out."

"Isn't that your vice-president's job?"

"I prefer to handle these matters myself."

"You need to learn to delegate."

"Delegate?" he repeated, scratching his head. "What's that?"

"Rafael, I'm serious. You deserve time off just like everyone else."

"And what do you suggest I do during this proposed time off?"

"Me!" she quipped, planting another quick kiss on his lips.

They exited the country club and admired the sprawling manicured grounds while they waited for the valet to bring Rafael's car from the parking lot. Seconds later, they were driving through the streets of Arlington, Virginia, listening to the radio and trading jokes.

"How long will you be at the office?" Paris asked, admiring his handsome profile. He still gave her butterflies, even after all these years, and she suspected that would never change. "Do you want me to come with you?"

"No, you need to rest. You've had a long week, and you deserve some R & R."

"Isn't that the truth!" Paris enjoyed being back in her hometown and loved spending time with Rafael, but working with her father day-in and day-out at their Washington headquarters was stressful. He was brisk with her, never satisfied and impossible to reason with. If not for Rafael, she'd be drowning her sorrows at the nearest bar. "Drop me off at the train station, and I'll take a cab back to the hotel."

"And risk some slick-talking businessman sweeping you off your feet? No way." Shaking his head as if he was trying to clear the image from his mind, he placed a hand on her leg and tenderly stroked her thigh. "I'm taking you to my place and that's final."

"My, my, aren't *we* bossy."

His laughter filled the car. "I admit it. I'm selfish. I want you all to myself."

You won't get any complaints from me, Paris thought, gazing adoringly at him. *I feel the same way, Rafael. I want to be with you and no one else.*

Paris opened the stainless-steel fridge, selected a bottle of white Zinfandel from the bottom shelf and strode down the darkened hallway, humming her favorite Miguel song. She'd spent the afternoon cooking and cleaning Rafael's bachelor pad and was anxiously awaiting his arrival. Wanting everything to be perfect for their romantic dinner, she polished the silverware, sprinkled red rose petals around the master bedroom and lit heart-shaped scented candles.

Paris caught sight of her reflection in the dresser mirror and paused to examine her appearance. Her hair was a mass of loose curls, her lips were red and glossy and her cleavage was perfect. Rafael had selected the white lace negligee yesterday at Discreet Boutiques, and Paris couldn't wait to see the look on his face when he saw her sexy ensemble.

At the thought of him, a girlish smile overwhelmed her mouth. Pulling back the curtains, she peeked out the window and glanced up and down the street. The sky was dark blue, filled with clouds and threatening evening showers. *What's taking him so long?* Paris wondered, for the umpteenth time, checking her diamond wrist watch. *He should have been home hours ago!*

Paris heard her BlackBerry ring, grabbed it off the dresser and put it to her ear. "Great timing, Kennedy. I was just thinking about you."

"You were supposed to call me back on Wednesday, but you never did. What gives?"

"Sorry, sis, but things have been crazy here for the past few days."

"Is work keeping you busy or that sexy new man of yours?"

Paris swallowed hard and licked her dry lips. "What are you talking about?"

"Don't play coy with me. I know all about you and Rafael Morretti."

"You do? Who told you?"

"Girl, please, pictures of you and that gorgeous heir are all over the gossip blogs."

"There are?" Stunned, Paris dropped into the tan armchair. "But we've been discreet."

"Kissing at major tourist attractions isn't exactly being discreet," Kennedy teased with a laugh. "Did you know he tweeted a picture of you guys at the White House?"

The news boggled her mind. "I didn't even know he had a Twitter account."

"Wait, there's more. Underneath the picture he wrote, 'Reunited and it feels so good'!"

Kennedy sighed dreamily, as if she was watching a love story on TV, and spoke with unbridled excitement. "I showed it to my coworkers, and they all oohed and ahhed. Paris, I'm so happy for you. You finally found a great guy. You. Go. Girl!"

Kennedy cheered, and Paris burst out laughing. Caught up in the moment, she spoke openly about her relationship with Rafael and told her sister about all the wonderful things he'd done for her over the past two weeks. Feeling guilty for monopolizing the conversation, Paris asked Kennedy about the kids and their fun-filled afternoon at the Georgia aquarium. "How is Anthony doing? Does he like his new job?"

"No, he hates it, but unfortunately he hasn't been able to find anything else."

"Talk to Dad," Paris advised, hoping her headstrong sister would finally take her advice. "We could use someone with Anthony's skill and expertise in our IT department."

"Speaking of Dad, have you told him you're dating someone?"

"No. The less he knows about Rafael the better. He's always believed the Morretti family was bad news, and once he gets something in his head it's hard to change his mind."

"Dad might disown you if he finds out you're seeing Rafael behind his back." Kennedy spoke in a soft, soothing tone, but her words were still a powerful blow. "You wouldn't be his favorite anymore. Could you handle that?"

As long as I have Rafael I have everything I need. The thought shocked Paris, but it was true. Deep down, she'd always dreamed of reuniting with her first love, and now that Rafael was back in her life she didn't want to ever let him go. What they had was special, rare, unlike anything she'd ever experienced and it was worth fighting for. "Can we *please* talk about something else?"

"Okay. What are you and the Italian stallion doing tonight?"

Despite herself, Paris laughed. "Don't call him that. His name is Rafael, and if you must know we're having a quiet, romantic dinner at home."

"That means you ordered Chinese takeout!"

"No, I cooked," she said proudly, admiring the spread on the candlelit table in the middle of the bedroom. "I made Caesar salad, tilapia with chili cream sauce and for dessert, Mom's German chocolate cake. *And* I made the icing from scratch."

Kennedy gasped.

"Oh, stop, you act like I don't cook."

"You don't, and never for dates, so you must really like Rafael."

I passed "like" a long time ago. I've fallen hard for him, and every day I find something new and wonderful to love about him.

"When are you coming home? Your nieces and nephews miss you, and so do I."

"Dad asked me to stick around until his assistant returns to work," Paris said, stealing another glance out the window. "We're working hard on several international projects, and if everything goes according to plan, Excel Construction will expand into the overseas market in 2020."

"Just make sure you're back in Atlanta in time for my anniversary party."

"Kennedy, we discussed this already."

"I know you have another engagement that night, but I'm hoping you'll change your mind. It would mean the world to me if you were there to celebrate with us."

"I'll try my best," Paris said quietly, touched by her sister's words.

"That's all I ask. Oliver is coming, and it would be great to see you both."

Paris heard the front door slam and jumped to her feet. "Honey, I'm home! Where are you?"

Her heart melted, and a soft sigh escaped her lips. Rafael's greeting was spoken in jest to make her laugh, but the longing in his voice made her feel like the most desirable woman in the world. "Kennedy, I have to go." Paris put on her high-heel shoes, straightened her negligee and fluffed her hair. "I'll call you tomorrow."

"Have fun, sis. I love you!"

Rafael strode into the bedroom, spotted her standing beside the window and frowned. "What's all this?" he asked, gesturing to the table. "Valentine's day isn't for another month."

"I know, but you're always doing sweet, romantic things for me, and I wanted to return the favor." Paris crossed the room and kissed him softly on the lips. "Do you like?"

"You have no idea." He took her hand in his, twirled her around and whistled. "If I knew you were waiting for me in this sexy getup, I would have been home hours ago!"

"Did everything go okay at the office? Is your security system back up and running?"

Rafael shook his head. "I don't want to talk about work. I want to talk about us."

"What's on your mind?"

He sat at the table, pulled her down on his lap and held her tight. "Coming home and seeing you here like this reminds me of the weekend we spent together in Cape May."

"I'm surprised you remember. That was eons ago."

"It was, but I never forgot how incredible it felt holding you and kissing you as we made love for the very first time. It is my most cherished memory."

His words left her speechless.

"Paris, I want you in my life, for the rest of my life." His fingertips caressed her cheek, her neck and her shoulders. "Tell me what I have to do to prove my love, and I'll do it."

"Rafael, what are you saying?" she asked, reuniting with her voice.

"I want you here with me, permanently, and I'll do whatever it takes to make you mine."

The candlelight cast a faint glow across his face, magnifying the intensity of his gaze. She saw the longing in his eyes, heard the vulnerability in his voice and melted in his arms. Something stirred inside her, but she tempered her enthusiasm. She'd been burned by love before and had promised herself the next time she met someone she would take things slow. So why was she considering his outrageous proposition after dating for only a few short weeks?

Because you've loved him since you were nineteen and nothing's changed! said her inner voice. *You can trust Rafael. He loves you and he'd never do anything to hurt you.*

"We just reconnected, and I live in Atlanta. Don't you think we're rushing things?"

"No, I don't. I don't believe in playing games or beating around the bush. I know what I want, Paris, and it's you." Excitement twinkled in his eyes, and he broke into a lopsided grin. "I'll come down to the ATL and help you pack. When's good for you?"

"Rafael, I'm serious."

"So am I. I mean every word." He tightened his hold around her waist and brushed his mouth against her neck and the delicate slope of her ear. "I took a risk opening up to you tonight, so promise me you'll give some thought to what I said."

Paris did. His words played in her mind for the rest of the night—during dinner, as they slow danced in the light of the moon and when they made love passionately in the shower—and the more she thought about his heartfelt declaration, the more excited she was about their future. Rafael was, and always would be, her first and only love, and she wasn't going to let fear control her life anymore—or her father.

Chapter 14

I haven't been this tired since my college days. Rafael swallowed a yawn and rubbed the sleep from his eyes. Waiting for the light to change at the busy downtown intersection, he took his cell phone out of his jacket pocket. He then reread the latest sexy, salacious text message he'd received from Paris. He'd dropped her off just moments ago at Excel Construction.

I'm feeling adventurous, so bring whipping cream, a blindfold and handcuffs when you come over tonight. I want to experiment in the bedroom. Are you up for a little role-playing?

Hell yeah! Reading the message made Rafael hot under the collar. Sweat clung to his Kenneth Cole suit and his heart pounded in his ears. He was desperate for her, desired her more than ever before. Paris was a woman of incredible beauty, intelligence and passion, and it didn't matter whether they were having drinks or making love, she always left him wanting more.

His thoughts returned to last night, and he replayed every minute of their impassioned encounter in her hotel suite. She'd whispered naughty words in his ear, moaned in pleasure with every grind, every urgent thrust. Paris made him feel whole, complete. They couldn't be more in sync, and although they'd been dating only a few weeks, Rafael was ready to make the ultimate commitment to her. His feelings for Paris were stronger than ever. They had a rock-solid relationship, and he loved the idea of her becoming his lawfully wedded wife.

He'd planned to be at Morretti Inc. bright and early that morning, but when Paris suggested they meet at the U Street Café, he'd readily agreed. They'd spent two hours talking and laughing over a luxurious breakfast. Thinking back on their time together made him grin from ear to ear. Every day with Paris was an adventure, an exciting new experience, and seeing her was the highlight of his day. They had dinner at noteworthy restaurants, danced for hours at trendy nightclubs, played miniature golf and had even recently ventured into paintballing. Paris got a kick out of shooting at him and cracked up every time he fell to the ground. Rafael had so many bumps and bruises it hurt to move, and as he crossed the street he felt sharp pains stab the back of his legs. *My dad was right,* he thought, trying not to limp, *a man in love will do anything for his woman, including make a complete and utter fool of himself.*

Rafael heard his cell phone chime and glanced at the screen to read his newest text. It was from Cicely. I need to see you. It's important. Without a second thought, he deleted the message and her phone number from his contact list. Rafael wanted nothing to do with her, and although he'd made it perfectly clear the last time they spoke, she continued calling and harassing him. He didn't want to have to get a restraining order against her, but if Cicely didn't stop blowing up his phone 24/7, that's exactly what he'd have to do.

Pulling up his jacket collar, he strode down the block toward his uncle Mario's jewelry store. Morretti Jewelers, a by-appointment-only boutique with a star-studded clientele, was located in a neighborhood overrun with cafés, art galleries and expensive restaurants. Shoppers crowded the streets, which were filled with laughter and animated conversation.

A bearded man wearing sunglasses and dark clothes bumped into Rafael and kept right on moving. No apology, no nothing. Rafael caught a glimpse of the stranger as he sped past, and a cold chill snaked down his spine. The guy looked like a heavier, darker version of Nicco's ex-best friend and former business partner, Tye Caldwell.

Rafael gave his head a hard shake, deleting the thought from his mind. He was seeing things. Had to be. No one had seen or heard from the shady businessman in months, and according to his family, he was backpacking through Eastern Europe.

Rafael stared through the crowd, hoping to get another look at the man, but he was long gone. As he continued up the block, Rafael made a mental note to call Gerald when he was finished shopping. *I'm probably being paranoid,* he thought, glancing over his shoulder once more, *but it wouldn't hurt to have Gerald do another background check on Tye.*

Rafael stopped in front of Morretti Jewelers and knocked on the glass. The door buzzed open. Lowering his head, he ducked inside the sleek, stylish store. Blinding white lights hung from the ceiling, glass cases filled with gems and jewels shimmered and sparkled and a mouth-watering aroma was heavy in the air. Rafael immediately spotted Demetri sitting in the waiting area and broke into a grin. His brother looked sharp in his white sweater and black dress pants, much older than his twenty-eight years, and debonair.

"Hey, bro, what's up?" Rafael bumped fists with him. "Where's Uncle Mario?"

"In the back on the phone. What took you so long? I've been waiting for almost an hour."

Noticing the empty plate on the round mahogany table, Rafael couldn't resist poking fun at his kid brother. "That's because you're greedy. You got here early to sample Aunt Rosetta's cooking, and from the looks of things you've been more than adequately fed!"

Demetri chuckled. "Guilty as charged. Aunt Rosetta can really throw down in the kitchen, and after my meeting at Washington Hospital, I was starving!"

"How did your appointment go?" Rafael peeled off his Burberry scarf and leather gloves. "What did Dr. Tanaka and his team say about your shoulder? Is it fully healed?"

His smile was proud. "Yup, I'm as good as new."

"That's great news. Congratulations. I know how hard you've worked in physical therapy to regain your strength, and I'm glad it paid off."

"Thanks, bro, and now that I have a clean bill of health from my surgeon I can finally return to the Cubs." His eyes were bright, filled with excitement. "Coach will probably limit my minutes the first few games, but I'm cool with that. As long as I can play, I'll be happy."

"I'm proud of you, Demetri. I hope you bat a thousand this season."

His brother gave a hearty laugh. "I have a better chance of meeting the president!"

"If you play hard the rest of the season you could definitely win another Sportsman of the Year award," Rafael said, unbuttoning his wool coat. "You can do it, bro. I have all faith in you. You're a Morretti *and* one of the best players in the league."

"I appreciate the vote of confidence." Demetri leaned forward in his chair and rested his arms comfortably on his legs. "I'm suiting up tomorrow against Washington, and I'm pretty stoked. You and Paris should come. I bet she'd love watching the game from the luxury box."

"We'll be there."

Demetri picked up his wineglass and took a drink.

"It's only eleven o'clock," Rafael said, pointing at the half-empty bottle of merlot. "Exactly how many glasses have you had?"

"Only three. I'm pacing myself!"

Rafael laughed and dumped his coat and scarf on a tan couch. He admired one of the cases filled with engagement rings, took his time studying and appraising each large, glittery diamond. As he made his way around the store his thoughts drifted back nine months. One afternoon, while shopping together at the mall, Cicely had dragged him into a ritzy jewelry store. In less than ten minutes she'd selected a diamond ring and somehow persuaded him to put down the 15 percent deposit. He'd never proposed, or ever given serious thought to popping the question. And as time went by Rafael realized that Cicely loved the Harry Winston diamond more than she loved him. He'd cared about her, but they weren't soul mates destined to be together. Their relationship had lacked fire and passion, but with Paris, he had it all. She was a spirited, vivacious beauty who loved life, her family and her community. If she accepted his marriage proposal next month he'd be the happiest man alive.

"Getting married is a big step."

"I know," Rafael conceded, nodding his head. "And I don't take it lightly. Mom and Dad have been married for thirty years, and I want to follow in their footsteps."

"You and Paris have only been dating for a few weeks—"

"But we've known each other for years. In fact, much, much longer than you've known Angela."

"I just don't want you to rush into anything."

Annoyed, Rafael shrugged off his brother's concerns. "I'm thirty-six, Demetri, not sixteen. This isn't puppy love. This is the real thing."

"Relationships are hard work, and you've never dated anyone longer than a few months," he pointed out. "Are you sure you know what you're doing?"

"I've never been more sure of anything in my life." Rafael faced his kid brother, looking him straight in the eye. "There's no doubt in my mind that Paris is the one for me. I felt it the first time I saw her, and even after fifteen years apart, nothing's changed. If anything, I love and respect her even more because I know she's a rare and precious find."

"That's beautiful, man." Demetri lowered his head and pretended to wipe a tear from his eye. "You really have a way with words, bro. Ever consider writing greeting cards?"

Rafael gave him a punch in the arm. "Knock it off or I'll tell Angela you dressed up as Miss Piggy in the tenth grade!"

"What? It was Halloween, and so did you!"

The men cracked up.

"I'm glad you and Paris reunited in Venice," Demetri said, his tone free of humor or amusement. "After all the stress and drama Cicely put you through, you deserve to be happy. I'm glad you found out the truth about her before it was too late."

Rafael nodded, thanked his lucky stars he'd called it quits just in the nick of time.

"Do Mom and Dad know about Paris?"

"No, not yet." Rafael wore a wry smile. "I can't wait to tell Mom I'm officially off the market. I love her dearly, but she's a terrible matchmaker, and bossy, too!"

Demetri laughed. "When are you going to pop the question?"

"Next month, on her thirty-sixth birthday. I already have everything planned. It's going to be a huge surprise, and I can't wait to see the look on Paris's face when I—"

"I thought you'd never get here!" Mario Morretti burst

into the store and strode toward Rafael with his hands out-stretched in greeting. "It's good to see you, son...."

Their uncle was a colorful character, with a booming voice and an energetic personality. Their dad had five younger brothers, but Mario had always been Rafael's favorite uncle. The loquacious jeweler was like a second father to him, and he often sought his advice when faced with tough decisions.

The men hugged, and Mario gestured to the back of the store with a flick of his head. "Are you hungry? I just finished having lunch with your aunt Rosetta, but there's plenty more food if you're interested."

"Thanks, Uncle, but I'm good."

"I want to hear all about your new girlfriend." He fervently nodded his head and rubbed his hands together. "The more I know about your fiancée-to-be, and you guys as a couple, the easier it will be for me to find the ring of her dreams."

Rafael didn't think long. "She's perfection," he said, as an image of Paris filled his mind. "Not only is she ridiculously beautiful, she's also passionate, down-to-earth and incredibly loyal. Her eyes are brighter than a million stars, her smile is infectious and her laugh is unlike anything I've ever heard. It's almost musical, and—" Rafael broke off speaking when he saw his uncle's jaw drop and his eyes triple in size. "What's the matter? What's wrong?"

Mario bumped elbows with Demetri. "You weren't kidding when you said Rafael was a goner! I've been in business for five decades and helped hundreds—" he frowned, gave his head a hard shake "—no, thousands of fellas buy engagement rings, but this is the first time I've ever seen a man gush!"

His uncle and brother erupted in laughter, and Rafael chuckled, too. He didn't mind his uncle poking fun at him. He was in love, had finally found the woman of his dreams after all these years of being deceived, and he wanted the world to know how much he loved his old college sweetheart. Paris was his everything, his destiny, and he couldn't be any happier.

Rap music exploded across the quiet boutique.

"That's my cell." Demetri fished his iPhone out of the back pocket of his blue jeans and checked the number on the screen. "I have to take this. It's Coach. I'll be right back."

Rafael took out his cell phone to check his email, but his uncle plucked it out of his hands and tossed it on the couch.

"Selecting an engagement ring takes both time and concentration, so we better get down to work." Mario clapped a hand on Rafael's shoulder and steered him toward the rear of the store. He joked, "If you can't find a ring in my boutique that your girlfriend will love, then it doesn't exist!"

Rafael took a seat across from his uncle at a round glass table. The sign hanging from the ceiling said The Platinum Collection, and as he peered inside the case he noticed every ring had a six-figure price tag.

"Do you already have something in mind?" Mario asked, setting a box of diamonds on the table. "A style or design she prefers, maybe?"

"No, but the bigger, the better."

"I know that," Mario drawled, wagging a plump finger in his nephew's face. "But I'm going to need a little more to go on. Does she like white gold, silver or yellow gold? What style does she prefer? Do you want a two-tone diamond or a single color? What shape and size?"

Rafael scratched his head. Who knew buying an engagement ring could be so stressful? Wasn't it supposed to be the easy part? His shoulders drooped and cold beads of sweat gathered on his forehead. He didn't want to buy the wrong ring, or worse, screw up the Valentine's Day proposal. He'd never popped the question before, and the thought of getting down on one knee and asking Paris for her hand in marriage made him feel nervous and excited at the same time. What if she turned him down? Or laughed in his face? What would he do if she rejected him?

"Would your girlfriend like this?"

The sound of Mario's loud, booming voice yanked Rafael out of his thoughts. "It's too old-fashioned," he said, glancing at the gold, vintage ring. "Definitely not her style. Paris is a modern woman with an eye for fashion, and—"

"Why didn't you tell me her name was Paris?"

Mario flapped his hands in the air as if he was batting away a pesky fly. And when his eyebrows climbed halfway up his broad forehead Rafael felt the urge to laugh.

"Her name tells me everything I need to know."

Mario locked the jewelry case and jumped to his feet. "I have the perfect ring," he promised, bustling around the counter. "Follow me to the back. The custom-made solitaire costs more than your Jaguar, but you're going to love it and so will she...."

"Where is it? Locked in the safe under heavy security?" Rafael joked, rising to his feet.

His uncle raised a bushy eyebrow. "Yeah, how did you know?"

The next hour was a blur, a whirlwind of conflicting thoughts and emotions. But when Rafael left Morretti Jewelers that afternoon with Demetri, carrying a velvet box wrapped with pink lace ribbon, he knew he was one step closer to making his dreams come true.

Chapter 15

"Paris, pick up the pace. This isn't Sweatin' for Seniors!" Mr. St. Clair snapped, raising his voice over the rock music playing on the radio in Excel Construction's fitness center. "Come on. You can do better than that...."

Groaning inwardly, Paris prayed her tired, aching legs wouldn't give way on the treadmill. Her chest was burning uncontrollably, and it hurt to breathe. Huffing and puffing, she gripped the front of the machine with one hand and wiped her forehead with the other. The ninth-floor fitness center inside the Washington headquarters of Excel Construction was filled with dozens of employees, but no one was exercising harder than her dad. Last year, after suffering a mild heart attack, he'd quit smoking, cleaned up his diet and adopted an intense fitness regimen. At sixty-one, Sebastian St. Clair was in the best shape of his life and had the muscles to prove it. He had the energy of a man half his age and loved to brag about his remarkable transformation.

"You're moving too slow. Increase your speed." Mr. St. Clair chugged a mouthful of Gatorade. "You're giving the keynote address at the Women's Business Expo in three days. Don't you want to look in tip-top shape?"

"Dad, I'm a senior executive, not Ms. Olympia 2014!"

Paris could think of a hundred things she'd rather do than exercise, but her dad had insisted. And since she wanted to talk to him privately, she'd reluctantly followed him to the spacious, brightly lit fitness center.

A Rashad J song came on over the speakers and a smile tickled her lips. Every time Paris heard "Between Your Thighs," the chart-topping single oozing with passion and sensuality, her thoughts turned to Rafael. When they weren't hanging out at his place, making dinner or cuddling on the couch, they were texting or video chatting. With Rafael, she felt the freedom to be herself— not the person her dad, her employees or her clients expected her to be—and Paris cherished every moment they spent together. Rafael was never too busy to see her, always lifted her spirits when she was having a bad day and never failed to make her laugh. He filled the emptiness in her life, gave her hope for a brighter tomorrow. There was nothing sexier than a sensitive, vulnerable man, and Paris found Rafael's honesty refreshing. More confident than ever, she was optimistic about her future and owed her new, improved outlook to her old college sweetheart.

Her eyes strayed to the wall clock above the glass door. At lunch, Rafael had called, sounding dreamy as usual, and asked her to meet him at his home at six o'clock. He had something up his sleeve; she could feel it, sense it, and could hardly wait to find out what it was. He spoiled her silly, did sweet, romantic things to brighten her day, and his thoughtfulness made Paris feel loved and adored.

"How are the plans coming along for the gala? Is everything booked and confirmed?"

Paris fanned a hand in front of her hot, clammy face. She was tired of jogging on the stupid machine and ready to hit the showers. Starving, with her stomach growling uncontrollably, she envisioned herself biting into a juicy cheeseburger, and hungrily licked her lips.

"Quit daydreaming," Mr. St. Clair snapped.

Blinking rapidly, Paris deleted the mouthwatering image from her mind. "Anthony and Kennedy are celebrating their sixteenth wedding anniversary in March."

"Good for them."

"They're throwing a party for their close friends and family in Atlanta at the Hyatt Hotel."

Her dad scowled. Sweat dribbled down his head and splashed onto his white Nike T-shirt. He was slim and of average height but had an imposing presence. "Is this conversation going somewhere or are you just shooting the breeze?"

Paris cleared her throat. "It's a big thing for Kennedy and Anthony, and I know it would mean the world to them if you were there."

"Your sister made her choice a long time ago, and I respect her decision."

"Dad, it's time to let go of the past."

"When I want your opinion, I'll ask you. Until then, zip it."

Paris exhaled, trying not to let his cold response dissuade her from speaking the truth. "Kennedy loves you, and she wants to have a better relationship with you."

"Then why are you telling me about the anniversary party?" he questioned, wiping his forehead with his white face towel. "Why didn't she call and invite me herself?"

Because Kennedy's just as stubborn and as bullheaded as you are! Paris studied her father, examining his profile. She detected a hint of sadness in his voice and felt a painful twinge inside her chest. Determined to get through to him, she stopped the treadmill and stepped off the machine.

"Drop it. I'm not going and there's nothing you can say to change my mind."

"You have three beautiful grandkids who never see

you...." Paris paused, giving her words time to sink in. "I think we should reschedule the charity gala and attend Kennedy and Anthony's anniversary celebration together...as a family."

"Absolutely not," he said, striking the treadmill with his fist. "I've already invited my friends and associates to the charity gala."

"But Kennedy's your daughter."

"It would be discourteous to cancel the event at the last minute."

"Says who?" Paris argued, growing frustrated. Their conversation was going nowhere, and she didn't have the energy to debate the issue with her father. Not after a punishing, hour-long workout. It was time to get back to work, and not a moment too soon.

"The charity gala will go ahead as planned, understood? Soldiers' Angels needs funds now more than ever, and I won't let them down."

"Charity should begin at home," Paris said, meeting his dark, angry gaze head-on. "That's what Mom used to say, and I think she was on to something. Kennedy doesn't need your money, Dad, she needs your love and support."

Sebastian coughed and lowered his head.

"If Mom was alive she'd be heartsick over the anger and animosity in this family." Her sorrow was suffocating, but Paris refused to bite her tongue. "I'm attending Kennedy and Anthony's anniversary party. They're my family, and I won't let them down."

Paris stuffed her iPod into her pocket and swiped her cell phone off the treadmill.

"What are you doing?" Mr. St. Clair asked, gesturing with his hands to the weight area. "We haven't done resistance training yet."

"Maybe next time." *Or never,* she thought, hustling toward the ladies' change room.

* * *

An hour later, Paris walked out of the fitness center feeling better than she had in weeks. Her thoughts were clear, her body was relaxed and she felt pretty in her fitted yellow dress.

Paris stepped off of the elevator, entered the lobby and gasped in surprise. Shocked to see Rafael standing at the front desk holding a massive bouquet of roses, she touched her stomach to still the butterflies swarming around inside. Though casually dressed in a navy blazer, argyle sweater and black slacks, he carried himself in a way that captured the attention of everyone around him. Rafael didn't just turn heads, he caused whiplash. The receptionist was making eyes at him, and so was every other woman in the lobby. Paris's heart swelled with pride. *That's right,* she thought, a smile exploding onto her lips. *My man's got it going on in more ways than one!* She fluffed her hair and exhaled a deep breath. Her legs felt like rubber, but she strode confidently through the lobby toward him.

"Rafael, hey, what are you doing here?" she asked, coming up behind him and touching his forearm. "I thought we were meeting at your place later tonight."

He kissed her on each cheek, allowing his lips to linger on her skin. Goose bumps exploded across her skin. Paris knew everyone in the lobby was watching them, but she gave Rafael a peck on the lips, anyway. *Damn, he tastes even better than he looks!*

"These are for you," he said, handing her the flowers.

"What's the occasion?"

"It's our two-month anniversary."

Paris buried her nose in the bouquet and inhaled the rich, fragrant scent.

"I want you to know how special you are."

He rested his hands on her waist, gently stroking and

caressing her hips. "I plan to be in your life for many years to come, so you better get used to me being around."

"Thank you, Rafael. This is a beautiful surprise."

"I know it isn't quitting time yet, but I was hoping I could persuade you to finish work earlier today," he said with a wink. "I want us to grab a bite to eat before the concert—"

"What concert?"

Rafael reached into his jacket pocket and took out two tickets. "I got front-row seats for the Backstreet Boys concert and passes for the after party at the Champagne Lounge."

"Shut up!" Paris cheered. "No way! I can't believe it!"

Rafael chuckled. "I take it you're pleased."

"Hell, yeah," she said with a laugh. "Kennedy tried to get us tickets for their Atlanta show last summer but by the time she got to Philips Arena it was sold out."

"I'm not surprised. I had to call in a bunch of favors to get these."

"I love you for it!"

Rafael wiggled his eyebrows. "You do, huh? Tell me more...."

Paris froze. Her heart leaped inside her throat. Rafael's smile couldn't be any bigger. Biting the inside her of cheek, she nervously shuffled her feet. She adored Rafael, but now wasn't the time to bare her soul.

"Is your father around? I'd like to give him my regards."

"Trust me, you don't. My dad isn't exactly a people person, and he can be very intimidating."

"We're going to get along great," Rafael said confidently. "We have a lot in common."

His words gave her pause. "You do?"

"Absolutely. We're both Georgetown University graduates, we run successful Fortune 500 companies, and I have a feeling you're the apple of his eye, too."

Her pulse beat loud and fast, and the urge to kiss him was all consuming. Paris wanted to dive into Rafael's arms and plant one on him, but she didn't want to cause a stir at Excel Construction.

"I'm going to go grab my things from my office. Wait right here," she said. "I know you're a ladies' man with a slick game, but try not to sweet-talk my employees while I'm gone, okay?"

"I only have eyes for you, and that will never change."

Be still my heart!

Paris spotted her father exiting the elevator and swallowed a groan. Panic rode inside her, filling her with a sickening sense of dread. *Something tells me this isn't going to be good,* she thought, clutching her flowers closer to her chest. Before she could even think of what to do, her dad was standing beside her, greeting Rafael as if they were old friends.

"It's been a long time. How are you doing?" Mr. St. Clair asked. "I trust that your parents and brothers are well."

"Everyone's great, sir, thanks for asking."

"Next time you speak to your father give him my best."

Rafael nodded. "Will do."

"I don't remember seeing your name on the client list this morning," Mr. St. Clair said, lines of confusion wrinkling his forehead. "Who are you meeting with today?"

Paris spoke up. "Dad, Rafael's not here on business. We have dinner plans tonight."

Her father's eyes doubled in size, and the color drained from his face.

"Don't worry, sir, I promise to have your daughter home before dark."

Paris felt relieved when she looked over and saw that her father was, too. *I was worried for nothing,* she decided, resisting the urge to do the happy dance up and down the lobby. *This is going better than expected. I can't believe it. My dad is actually smiling!*

"I'm going back to my office." Mr. St. Clair adjusted his pin-striped tie and ran a hand over his tailored suit jacket. "Have a good time tonight and be safe."

"Thank you, sir. It was great seeing you again. Take care."

Paris snapped out of her thoughts. "Rafael, I'll be right back."

"Take as long as you need. I'm not going anywhere."

His words and his piercing gaze gave her a rush. Paris strode out of the lobby and hurried to her corner office as fast as her feet could take her. Her father was hot on her heels, marching briskly behind her, speaking in a hushed tone.

"We need to talk."

"Not now, Dad. Rafael's waiting."

Paris threw open her office door and rushed inside. It was a gorgeous space, filled with sunshine, art and cushy furniture. Bookshelves lined the walls, framed photographs of her nieces and nephews decorated her desk and fresh air drifted in through the open window.

"How long have you been cavorting with Rafael Morretti?"

His question threw her. "Dad, I've known Rafael since college. You know that," she said, resting her bouquet on the desk. "He's a perfect gentleman and one of the most thoughtful people I have ever met."

"It would be unwise to date someone with ties to the Italian Mafia. It could be asking for trouble." Sebastian's gaze was cold and challenging, and his arms were folded rigidly across his chest. "His father, Arturo Morretti, is an unscrupulous businessman, and I suspect the apple didn't fall far from the tree. Didn't you learn anything from your last relationship?" His face clouded with anger, and his tone now filled with disgust. "That dreadful fiasco with Winston should have made you smarter about men and relationships."

Paris didn't want to think about the day her ex-boyfriend died or the emotional breakdown she'd suffered at his funeral. It was times like this, when her father threw her mistakes in her face, that she feared she'd never escape her past or live down what she'd done.

"Men like Rafael Morretti can't be trusted."

Anger bubbled inside her, but she didn't lose her temper. "Rafael doesn't have ties to the Mafia or any other criminal organization. His ex-girlfriend started that rumor to get back at him for dumping her, and I know for a fact that it isn't true."

"Is that so?"

"Rafael is a man of character and integrity, and as by-the-book as they come. He's never even had a parking ticket, for goodness' sake!"

"Open your eyes," Mr. St. Clair exclaimed through clenched teeth. "He's using you."

"Using me? That's ludicrous. What for?"

"Isn't it obvious? Surely you can't be *that* dumb."

His words were a slap to the face, a painful, crushing blow Paris never saw coming. Her feelings were hurt, but she concealed her emotions. Questions stormed her mind, one after another. Was Rafael right? Was it time she put her foot down and regained control of her life?

"I won't stand by and let you soil my good name by dating *that* man."

"Dad, lower your voice," she whispered, glancing at the open door. "You're yelling."

"Of course I'm yelling! You're running around town with a shady businessman!"

Paris felt a scowl twist her lips. She loved her father dearly, even when he was being unreasonable, but she'd had enough of his insults for one day. Thanks to Rafael she was happier than she'd been in years, and for the first time in her life she didn't care what her dad thought.

"Cancel," Mr. St. Clair demanded. "I mean it, Paris. Get out there and do it right now, or you're going to see a real ugly side to me."

In that moment, Paris realized everything Kennedy had ever said about their father was true. He wanted to control her, like a puppet, and was determined to run every aspect of her life. Paris knew then, with all certainty, that if she didn't stand up to him things would never change.

"This conversation is over," she said calmly, ignoring the nervous quaver in her voice. "I don't need nor want your advice, and I'd appreciate if you kept your opinions to yourself."

"Watch your tone. I am your father and you will respect me."

"Respect goes both ways." Paris picked up her purse. "Dad, I love you, and I appreciate all the sacrifices you've made for me, but I won't let you run my life anymore."

"Who the hell do you think you're talking to? This is my business—"

"And this is *my* life," she retorted. "I decide who to date, not you."

Then Paris did something she'd never done before. She snatched her blazer off the coatrack and walked out on her father.

Chapter 16

"That's the last time I take *you* to see the Backstreet Boys," Rafael teased, playfully wiggling his eyebrows. "You screamed so loud during the concert I *still* can't hear in my left ear!"

"I know you're not talking," she quipped. "You were singing and dancing, too. Don't even try to deny it, because I recorded you on my cell phone!"

Laughing, they clinked wineglasses and shared a sweet kiss.

Cheers exploded inside the Champagne Lounge. The restaurant had the ambience of a high-end nightclub, and the enchanting music, sultry lights and vintage decor made the establishment a hit among the over-thirty crowd. Decorated in copper and ivory hues, the two-story building was the epitome of class and sophistication. The atmosphere in the bar was cheerful, the food was exceptional and the aromas wafting out of the kitchen were intoxicating.

Paris grooved to the R and B song the live band was playing, rocking her shoulders and hips to the beat of the soulful music. The Champagne Lounge was her favorite place to relax at the end of a long workday, and although her argument with her father earlier was still heavy on her mind, she was having a great time with Rafael. They were sitting side by side in their cozy leather booth, holding hands and sharing kisses. *This is heaven,* she thought, snuggling up to her handsome date. *What more could a girl want?*

"Do you want to get your picture taken with the Backstreet Boys?" Rafael asked.

From their corner booth, Paris could see a long line of attractive women waiting outside the VIP area. She marveled at how giddy and excited they seemed. "I'm a fan, not a groupie," she said. "I'm fine right here with you, thank you very much."

He pressed his lips to her cheek. "Good answer."

Paris giggled when Rafael nuzzled his face against her neck. He was full of surprises, both in and out of the bedroom, and she was eagerly looking forward to returning to his place. Her heart overflowed with happiness when he kissed her, and desire warmed her skin as his hands caressed her legs. Instinctively, she arched her body toward him, moving in close. "I had an amazing time tonight," she said, gazing deep into his eyes. "Thanks for taking me to see my all-time favorite boy band. It was a wonderful surprise."

"I wish you didn't have to go back to Atlanta." Rafael took her hand in his and gently caressed her fingertips. "Are you sure you can't stick around a few more days?"

"I can't. I've already extended my trip once. If I miss Kennedy and Anthony's anniversary bash next weekend they'll never forgive me."

"Can I be your date? I don't know if you've noticed, but I clean up pretty good."

"Oh, I noticed," she said, in a singsong voice. "And so did every woman in here. You caused quite a stir when you entered the restaurant, Mr. Morretti."

"That's because *you* were on my arm."

Paris laughed. "Aren't you going to Miami to visit your family?"

"Yes, and I want you to come with me."

Shocked and confused by his words, she gave him a blank look.

"We can spend a week with my family in the Magic City, then head to Atlanta for your sister's anniversary party. Sound like a plan?"

"Meeting your family is a big step," she reluctantly said.

"I know, but I'm ready to take things to the next level, and I hope you are, too."

"Aren't you worried about giving your mom and dad the wrong impression?"

"Paris, my parents know all about you."

His words stole her breath. "They do?"

"Yeah, I spilled the beans last weekend when they drove in from New York." He brushed an errant strand of hair away from her face and wore an impish smile. "My father Google searched you on his cell and was impressed with your bio on the Excel Construction website."

A smile claimed her lips. Paris was proud of what she'd accomplished at her father's company. Although being a senior executive wasn't her dream job, she always strived to do her best.

"My mother thinks you're a beautiful, accomplished woman, and I have to agree," Rafael said.

"Did your mom like Cicely? Were they close?" Paris blurted out.

"They never met."

"But you guys dated for almost a year."

Rafael shrugged a shoulder. "I know, but we were never that serious."

Questions rose in her thoughts, rousing her curiosity. Paris started to speak, but lost her train of thought when she spotted a familiar face at the bar. It was a man from her past, someone she hadn't seen in years, and he was staring at her with a cold, fixed regard. A violent shiver tore through her body. *Oh, no, what is he doing here? And why is he giving me the evil eye?*

Guilt was a tricky emotion. Paris had done nothing wrong, but she felt guilty for sitting with Rafael in the Champagne Lounge. The waiter arrived, asking if she wanted another strawberry mojito, but Paris didn't speak. Memories of sobbing mourners, a gray casket and an inconsolable widow invaded her thoughts. A bitter taste filled her mouth, one so thick and acrid, she felt sick to her stomach. It hurt to breathe, to swallow, and all she could think about was that fateful night in January, three years earlier.

"Baby, are you okay? You look like you've seen a ghost."

Rafael took her hand. His question was met with silence. He heard Paris sniffle, then saw her eyes cloud with tears. He struggled to make sense of how their intimate conversation had taken such a drastic turn for the worse. Following the route of her gaze, he scrutinized the dark-skinned man in the striped shirt and black pants. He looked smooth, like the kind of brother who could talk himself out of any situation. Though a scantily dressed woman hung from his arm, his eyes were on Paris, sharper than laser beams, and a sneer twisted his lips.

"I have to get out of here. Can we go now? Please?"

"Sure, let me just pay the tab."

Rafael took out his wallet, dropped five hundred dollars on the table and stood. Offering his hand, he helped Paris to her feet and then led her through the crowded dining area. They walked out of the restaurant and past the long line of people waiting behind the red velvet rope.

"It's a gorgeous night," he said, holding her close to his side. "Let's walk down First Street. I have something to show you."

They strode down the block, past high-end department stores, five-star hotels and luxury apartment buildings. Rafael was lost in his own troubling thoughts. He wanted to ask Paris about the gentleman back at the bar, but sensed it was not the right time. Her eyes were sad and she seemed as if she were in another world. Very unlike her. One of the things Rafael loved most about Paris was her zest for life and her ability to laugh at any situation. He hated to see her upset.

They stopped in front of a vacant store with a For Rent sign in the window. Rafael took a key out of his pocket and unlocked the door. He flipped on the lights and led Paris inside. The air held the faint scent of perfume, and the gleaming, hardwood floors were so clean Rafael could see his reflection. The store was bright and spacious, bursting with possibility, and the vibrant cranberry walls were eye-catching.

"This is a great real estate investment, and since my cousin Dante owns the building I know he'll give you a fair price."

"Me?" Her eyes widened. "I'm not interested in buying commercial property."

"Yes, you are. You're going to open a full-service beauty salon called Beauty by Paris St. Clair, and it's going to be a hit." Rafael spread his hands in front of him to paint the picture. "I can see it now. Customers lined up around the block, women eating biscotti and sipping merlot in the waiting area and old school jams playing on the stereo."

Paris laughed. "I know that's right!"

"The property has been vacant for several months, and my cousin is desperate to get it off his hands," he explained. "If you'd like I could set up a meeting with Dante later this week."

"But this is a long way from home."

"Would you relocate for love?"

Her eyes darted away from his face, wandered aimlessly around the vacant store. The tone of her voice concerned him. Paris sounded unlike herself, quiet and emotional, as if she was going to burst into tears at any moment.

"Before New Year's Eve we hadn't seen each other in fifteen years."

"I know," he conceded, nodding his head. "We have a lot of catching up to do."

"I'm scared of rushing things. We haven't been dating long—"

Rafael stepped forward, until they were face-to-face, and cradled her cheeks in his palms. "But I've loved you for years," he whispered, desperate to get through to her. "You are and always will be the only woman for me, and nothing will ever change that."

He kissed the corners of her lips, allowing his hands to stroke and caress her soft, warm flesh. "I'm ready to commit to you Paris…mind, body and soul."

"I need more time…."

"How much? In case you haven't noticed, I'm not getting any younger."

A laugh fell from her lips. "Your biological clock is keeping you up at night, too, huh?"

Rafael cracked up. *There* was the woman he knew and loved. He enveloped her in a hug and kissed her forehead. Paris had all the qualities he was looking for in a partner. He wanted to be the only man who made her smile, the only man she kissed and loved. Deep in his heart he felt that his old college sweetheart was the woman he was destined to marry.

"What happened back at the Champagne Lounge?" he asked, his curiosity finally getting the best of him. "Why were you so upset?"

Paris left the comfort of his warm arms and wandered over to the front window. She stared outside into the darkness, and when she spoke her voice sounded hollow, lifeless. "I saw someone from my past who brought back bitter memories."

"Was the guy at the bar an old lover?"

"God, no," she said, shaking her head. "He's my exboyfriend's brother."

Rafael walked over to the window. He didn't want to upset her, but he needed to know the truth about her past relationship. And more important, if she was still in love with her ex-boyfriend. Rafael knew Paris would never intentionally hurt him—not like the cold, calculating women he'd dated in the past—but he'd been burned before and was determined to be smart this time around. Her birthday was fast approaching but Rafael wanted to get everything out in the open before he popped the question. "Are you and your ex-boyfriend still close?" he asked, trying to sound calm, despite his nerves.

"He died three years ago in a motorcycle accident."

Rafael rested a hand on her shoulder. He wanted to take her in his arms, to kiss the track of her tears, but sensed she needed a private moment with her thoughts. "I'm sorry for your loss."

"The first few months after Winston passed were tough, but thanks to the support of my family and friends I'm in a much better place now."

"What was he like? Was he good to you?"

Paris appeared hesitant. "Winston was a fun, spontaneous guy who lived life to the fullest," she said, wearing a sad smile. "Everyone loved him and thought we made a great couple. Three months into our whirlwind courtship our relationship turned into a nightmare."

Intrigued, Rafael felt his curiosity stir. "What happened?"

"I found out Winston wasn't the man I thought he was. Not by a long shot."

Paris took a deep breath. As her confession unfolded, tears welled up in her eyes. "Two days after Winston's motorcycle accident, I discovered he wasn't the affluent, well-connected attorney he appeared to be. He wasn't a Princeton graduate, and he was ten years older than me, not five. He was living a double life that I knew nothing about, but that wasn't the worst of it."

Paris hugged her arms to her body. "At the funeral, I found out Winston was married. His wife gave the eulogy, and when she called him her one true love I burst into tears…."

Rafael took her in his arms and tenderly caressed her.

"I shouldn't have been so trusting. I should have checked him out."

"Paris, you did nothing wrong."

"But I picked him. I willfully chose to be with him," she argued, her words a breathless whisper. "What does that say about me as a person? What does that say about my character?"

Rafael gave a solemn nod. "I questioned my judgment after Cicely betrayed me, too. I was embarrassed and felt like an ass for getting played for a fool."

"I know just how you feel." Paris raised her eyes to his face and spoke in a quiet voice. "How did you overcome her betrayal? How did you learn to forgive yourself and move on?"

"My brothers sat me down and talked some sense into me."

He chuckled at the memory of his kid brothers barging into his Georgetown home and sitting him down at the kitchen table. "They encouraged me to focus on the future, not the past, and reminded me of my value and self-worth," he said, his tone strong and unwavering. "What they said hit home. Having their support made a world of difference, and once I stopped beating myself up, it was easy to forgive myself and move on."

Paris sniffed, absently twisting the diamond ring on her left hand.

"Did your ex-boyfriend give you that ring?"

"No," she said. "I bought it a couple years ago when I was in France on business."

"To keep the opposite sex from getting too close, right?"

"No, I just love Cartier diamonds," she said with a smile.

"That's a lie and you know it, Paris."

His gaze zoomed in on her, held her in its seductive grasp. Paris sucked in a mouthful of air, and Rafael saw that she was shaking.

"Paris, you'll never have to worry about me betraying you."

"Love doesn't last," she argued. "At least not for me."

"Don't say things like that. It's not true."

"Yes, it is. I'm thirty-five years old, and I've never had a successful long-term relationship...." She trailed off, seeming to take a moment to gather her thoughts.

He took her hands, gripping them tightly. "I don't know what the future holds, Paris, but I do know this.... I love you with everything I am, and that will never change."

"What if things don't work out? What if we end up hurting each other?"

"I understand your apprehension but you have nothing to fear. Fate reunited us for a reason, and I won't give up on us." His stare was bold and his tone filled with determination. "In Venice you asked me to trust you, and now I'm asking you to trust me."

When Rafael tightened his hold, her eyes glimmered with tears again.

"Paris, give me a chance to prove I'm worthy of your love...."

A smile broke out through her tears, and she slowly nodded. "Okay."

"Okay?" he repeated, raising an eyebrow. "Does that mean you'll be my boo?"

"How can I refuse? You're a great guy, an amazing lover and you like the Backstreet Boys!"

They shared a laugh and held each other close.

"Can I have a kiss?" he asked, flashing a boyish smile.

Paris draped her arms around his neck. "I thought you'd never ask."

Chapter 17

Hump day was kicking Rafael's butt, and there wasn't a damn thing he could do about it. Shaking off his fatigue, he straightened in his leather executive chair and took a swig of his coffee. Reviewing profit reports, back-to-back meetings and video conference calls with overseas clients left him feeling drained.

Rafael was looking forward to his trip to Miami on Friday for more reasons than one. He was excited about Paris finally meeting his parents, and spending some quality time with his family. He planned to meet with detectives next week and hoped they'd made more progress with the arson investigation. Rafael had used Skype to talk to his brothers yesterday, and thankfully, they had nothing suspicious or worrisome to report. Things were quiet in Miami, and that was a very good thing. Nicco and Demetri were busy with their wives-to-be, and when their conversation turned to wedding plans, he'd taken notes instead of rolling his eyes. He'd be planning his own wedding in the near future, so why *not* start doing his homework now?

Rafael dropped his pen on his desk and scooped up his phone. *I need a break, and I know just who to call.* He punched in Paris's cell number and waited for the call to connect. Just the thought of her excited him, and the moment her bubbly, effervescent voice filled the line his stress evaporated and his spirits lifted.

"Have I told you lately that I love you?" Rafael sounded

more like Kermit the Frog than Rod Stewart, but he sang his favorite song—the one that made him think of his college sweetheart—with great conviction and feeling.

Paris clapped and cheered enthusiastically. "Oh, baby, that was great! Sing it again!"

Chuckling, he shook his head. Leave it to Paris to make him laugh. It didn't matter how tired or how stressed out he was, talking to his lady love always made him feel a hundred times better. "Today's the big day," he said, leaning back comfortably in his chair. "Are you nervous?"

"You have no idea. My hands are shaking so hard I can't apply my mascara!"

"Baby, you have nothing to worry about. You're going to knock 'em dead this afternoon at the expo, and I'll be there to cheer you on."

Paris groaned. "Now I'm *really* nervous."

"Don't be. You've practiced your speech a million times, and it's one of the best I've ever heard. You've got this, Paris. You can do it," he exclaimed. "And after your speech I'm taking you to the Capital Grille for a celebratory dinner."

"Don't you have a board meeting tonight?"

"Attending the Women's Business Expo is important to me, so I gave myself the night off and asked my VP to take my place."

"Really?" Her tone was one of disbelief. "That's so unlike you."

Turning toward the window, he admired the view. The sky was free of clouds and a rich shade of blue. The sun was blinding—much like Paris's smile—and filled his office with warmth and light. Rafael thought of Venice, of the time he'd spent sightseeing with her at Saint Mark's Square, and recalled their conversation at the gelato shop.

"A wise young woman once said, 'The purpose of life is to live it, to taste adventure and excitement to the utmost and to reach out eagerly and without fear for newer and richer experiences.' And I've taken her words to heart. I don't want to work 24/7 anymore, or spend weekends at home with my dogs. I want to experience all that life has to offer."

Paris gasped. "Wow, I can't believe it. You really *do* listen to me!"

"Of course I do. You're smart, insightful and gorgeous, too."

"Keep talking," she quipped, her tone thick and sultry. "I'm listening.…"

"You're special to me, and I'll do anything to make you happy."

"I feel the same way, Rafael. I'm committed to this relationship. I want us to work."

"We will," he said confidently. "I'm certain of it."

"I love when you sound all macho. It's *such* a turn-on."

Her words made him feel ten feet tall.

"We better get off the phone before things go from PG to X-rated," she joked with a laugh. "My driver will be here in fifteen minutes and I'm still not dressed."

"Wear your red Chanel suit." He added, "And leave your panties at home."

Paris squealed.

"Okay, bye beautiful. See you in a bit," he said with a grin.

Chuckling to himself, Rafael hung up the phone. Feeling energized, he flipped open his leather-bound portfolio and scooped up his pen. For the rest of the morning, he worked diligently to finish his paperwork. He blocked out the ringing telephones and the high-pitched laughter outside his office door and focused his energy on the task at hand.

Minutes turned to hours. By the time his executive assistant, Nia Patrick, popped her head inside his office door at noon, he was finished his to-do list and reviewing his agenda for his upcoming business trip to Dubai.

"I'm going to the corner deli to grab lunch," she said, tapping her long, thin fingers against the wall. "I'll get you combo number six and those chocolate macadamia nut cookies you love so much. Anything else?"

"No, nothing for me, thanks."

Frowning, she tilted her head and studied him over the rim of her designer eyeglasses. "But it's Wednesday. You always have the squash soup and chicken panini."

Rafael opened his briefcase and put his electronic notebook inside. "I don't have time. I'm leaving at two o'clock, and I won't be coming back for the rest of the day."

"No problem. I'll forward important calls and emails to your cell phone."

"No. Don't." Rafael saw her eyes widen, and felt guilty for snapping at her. "I'll be at the Business Women's Expo this afternoon, and I don't want to be disturbed."

"The Women's Business Expo?" she repeated, a bewildered expression on her face. Nia entered the office, closed the door behind her and cautiously approached his desk. "Forgive me for speaking out of turn, but is everything okay?"

Amused, Rafael abandoned his search for his WiFi pen and gave the brunette his undivided attention. "Everything's great. Why do you ask?"

"Because you've been acting strange ever since you returned from Venice eight weeks ago…. I think you should talk to someone."

"Like a therapist?"

Nia snapped her fingers. "That's a great idea, and I think it would be most beneficial," she said, fervently nodding her head. "Do you want me to make some calls?"

"No, thank you."

"Well, I'm worried about you." Her eyes filled with

concern. "I'm not trying to scare you, Mr. Morretti, but you're exhibiting the telltale signs of someone experiencing a nervous breakdown."

Laughter exploded from Rafael's mouth. His executive assistant was a riot. As with Paris, Rafael could always count on Nia to make him laugh. "I appreciate your concern, but I'm fine. Great, actually." He smiled at her, attempting to put her overactive mind at ease. "I'm taking Paris out for dinner after the conference and if I eat a big lunch it will ruin my appetite."

"You're seeing Paris St. Clair again?" Nia looked awestruck. Her hazel eyes were big and bright. "You've seen her every day this week. Wow, you must *really* like her!"

"You better get going or you'll get stuck in the lunch rush."

His assistant spun on her heels. "Danica Lyons will be here at one o'clock, but I should be back before she gets here," she said as she breezed through the door.

To kill time, Rafael logged in to his email account. He looked at the pictures from the Backstreet Boys concert and smiled as the images filled his computer screen. In some photographs, Paris was making faces; in others she was laughing or blowing him kisses.

"Hi, Rafael. It's been a long time."

The hairs on the back of his neck shot up. His eyes slid to his office door, and when his gaze landed on Cicely, a curse fell from his mouth. His ex-girlfriend was standing beside the bamboo plant, wearing a tentative smile and fussing with her white ruffled scarf. Her face was fuller than he remembered, and her pixie hairstyle suited her nicely. Cicely did whatever it took to look like a VIP, regardless of the staggering cost.

Rafael hadn't seen her in months. Not since she gave that tell-all interview to *Celebrity Scoop* and he had no desire to speak to her. Especially not after all the malicious lies she'd said about him. "Leave or I'll call security."

"Don't be like that," she said, as if she were admonishing an errant child. "After dating for almost a year I'd like to think we could have a civil conversation about our future."

"What future?" he asked, shooting her a disgusted look. The aspiring actress was delusional, so he adopted a no-nonsense tone and gave it to her straight. "I've moved on, and you should, too."

"You'll never find someone who loves you as much as I do."

"Thank God for that," he mumbled, logging off of his computer.

"Can I come in? We really need to talk."

"No, you can't. We're over, and there's no way in hell I'm taking you back, so—"

"You might after you hear what I have to say."

Rafael gave his ex-girlfriend a bewildered look. The notion of him reuniting with Cicely was laughable. He wanted to be with someone loyal and trustworthy, not an immature, attention-seeking girl. He had no desire to rekindle their flame. He had Paris now, and he didn't need or want anyone else. "Please leave," he said, struggling to control his temper. "I need to prepare for my next meeting, and my client should be here any minute now."

"Danica Lyons isn't coming."

"What do you know about Ms. Lyons?"

"I knew you'd never agree to see me, so I asked Danica to call on my behalf," she said, inspecting her manicure. "Danica is in my acting class, and we've become good friends over the past few months. When I told her my story, she agreed to help."

Rafael felt his eyelids thin and his nostrils flare. "You're something else, you know that?"

"What was I supposed to do? I was trying to be reasonable, but you left me no choice." Cicely's voice was strained, and she flailed her hands in the air. "You won't return my calls. And the last time I was here you refused to see me."

"I don't need this." Rafael scooped up the phone, pressed 9 and put the receiver to his ear. The sooner he got rid of Cicely, the better. His patience was growing thin, and he worried about doing something he'd regret. "I'm calling security. You can tell *them* your sob story while they escort you out of the building."

Rafael expected Cicely to turn around and storm out of his office, but she didn't move. She unbuttoned her jacket and when Rafael saw her burgeoning belly, the phone slipped from his grasp and dropped to his desk with a clang.

"That's right," she said matter-of-factly. "I'm eight months pregnant with your child."

Chapter 18

Rafael stared at Cicely with hard-eyed scrutiny. Disgust seeped into his pores, filled him with anger. Her words haunted him, echoed over and over in his mind.

Pressing his eyes shut, he shook his head. Rafael didn't believe Cicely knew without a shadow of a doubt that he was the father of her child. And as he listened to her complain about how awful her pregnancy was, he wondered if she'd concocted this scheme with her crafty mother.

Rafael heard a male voice fill the air and snatched up the phone.

"Hello? Mr. Morretti? Can you hear me?"

He quickly assured the security guard that everything was okay and hung up.

"Congratulations on your pregnancy," Rafael said. "I wish you nothing but the best."

"That's it? That's all you have to say?"

He gave her a blank stare. *What did I ever see in her? How could I have ever dated this scheming, manipulative woman for nearly a year?* They'd met at the dog park, and while walking along the trails with their pets, discovered they had shared interests and hobbies. He'd been drawn to her bold personality, and in many ways she had reminded him of his old college sweetheart. Both women were strong, outgoing beauties who could light up any room. But that was where the similarities ended. Paris put her friends and family first—above anything else—

but Cicely didn't have a loyal bone in her body. All she cared about was being famous, and she'd con—or betray—anyone to make it happen.

"We were never exclusive," he reminded her. "And you started dating an NFL player a few days after we broke up, remember?"

Cicely shrugged. "I'm a single girl with needs. I'll do what I have to do."

"Then I suggest you contact your ex, because I am not your baby's father."

"I'm due next month, which means I conceived sometime last summer before we broke up," she explained, her voice filled with pride. "Do the math. You'll see that I'm right."

"I don't believe you, and don't think for a second that your pregnancy changes things. It doesn't. I'm dating someone and I won't let you come between us."

A sneer claimed her lips. "I almost fell over when I saw pictures of you and that woman in *The Washington Post*." Jealousy showed on her face and seeped into her tone. "I don't know what you see in her. She's fake and pretentious, and from what I've heard a real—"

Rafael silenced her with a glare. "Don't go there."

"All I'm saying is she's *not* all that."

"She. Is." Arguing with Cicely was beneath him, but he felt compelled to defend the woman he loved. Paris was his world, his everything, and he wasn't going to let Cicely bash her. "Paris St. Clair is more woman than you'll ever be," he said, bursting with pride "She's smart, successful, beautiful and loyal."

"Oh, please. Get your head out of the clouds. No one's *that* great."

"Paris is." Talking about his girlfriend made him feel on top of the world. "You know what I admire most about her? She's an independent woman who doesn't need me or anyone else to take care of her. That's damn sexy if you ask me."

"Good for her," Cicely mumbled, making herself comfortable in one of the armchairs in front of his desk. "I didn't come down here to listen to you gush about how great your new girlfriend is. I came down here to talk about the well-being of our child."

"I'm not the father," he said, tired of repeating himself. "I always use protection."

As the words left his mouth, his mind flashed back to New Year's Eve. He'd had unprotected sex only once in his life—with Paris—and as the memories of that night washed over him his temperature soared. His desire for her was insatiable.

"The only surefire protection against unwanted pregnancies is abstinence," Cicely preached. "I'm 100 percent certain you're the father. A DNA test will prove it."

The thought froze in his brain, obliterating every other one in his mind. Cicely sounded confident, looked it, too. *Damn, what if I am the father?* Panic rose inside the walls of his chest, and fear spread through his veins. His throat closed up, making it impossible to speak, to breathe. *How would Paris feel about me being a father? Would a baby be a deal breaker?*

Hell, yeah, his conscience answered. *There's no way in hell she'd stay with you!*

Rafael pressed his eyes shut and pushed the thought to the furthest corner of his mind. He wasn't losing Paris again, and since he wasn't the father of Cicely's baby he had nothing to worry about. His heart quit pounding in his ears and his breathing slowed.

"I've been too sick to go on auditions, and my savings are running out...." *She paused.* "As the baby's father, it's your responsibility to take care of my financial needs. If you don't, I'll go public with my story."

"Are you blackmailing me?"

"I am doing what's best for me, and *our* baby."

"I don't owe you anything," he snapped. "This conversation is over. Please leave. From now on you can reach me through my attorney."

"Rafael, please, I'm…desperate," Cicely whined. "I only have a couple hundred dollars left in my bank account."

"Then ask your mother or one of your boyfriends for help."

"I can't. I'm too embarrassed."

Convinced she was giving an Oscar-worthy performance to gain his sympathy, he asked the question on the tip of his tongue. "What happened to the money you got from *Celebrity Scoop* magazine? I heard they paid you very well for the interview you gave about me."

Shame clouded her eyes. "Rafael, I never meant to hurt you."

"Then why did you slander my family in a national magazine?" he demanded, giving a voice to his anger. "I trusted you, Cicely, and you made me look like a fool."

"It wasn't my idea," she argued, her tone a desperate plea. "My mom contacted the magazine and gave the interview on my behalf."

"I don't believe you."

"I don't expect you to, but it's the truth."

Rafael narrowed his eyes. "How did the magazine get all those pictures of us if you had nothing to do with the interview?"

"My mom must have gotten them from my cell phone when I wasn't paying attention."

"You have an answer for everything, don't you?"

Her teardrop earrings tinkled when she shook her head. "It's not like that, Rafael. I'm not the monster you think I am. I had nothing to do with the exposé, I swear."

Rafael didn't know what to think, what to believe. He

released a deep sigh and raked a hand over his hair. Cicely was a liar, a master manipulator, but his immediate gut feeling was that she was telling the truth. She wasn't a bad person, just misguided. Her screwed-up relationship with her mother had everything to do with her selfish, materialistic ways.

"I don't want there to be any animosity between us," she said in a soft tone. "We're having a baby, and I want to raise our child in a two-parent home...."

Rafael gripped his armrest, clutching it so tightly his knuckles throbbed. He wanted to yell at Cicely, to call her every name in the book, but realizing there was nothing to gain from being petty and vindictive, he swallowed his retort.

"Are you willing to take a paternity test?"

The question caught him off guard. He could do the DNA test on Friday, before he left with Paris for Miami, but he didn't share his thoughts with Cicely quite yet. He didn't trust her. He worried if he told her about his plan, she'd show up at the hospital. Rafael couldn't let his ex-girlfriend worm her way back into his life. He'd take the test alone, on his terms, or not at all.

"We can have it done this afternoon at Washington Medical," she proposed, her eyes bright with excitement. "The sooner the better, don't you think?"

"I can't. I already have plans."

"Okay, then, I guess I'll just take my check and be on my way."

Rafael opened his side drawer and stared at his checkbook. Conflicted, he struggled with what to do. What if Cicely was telling the truth? What if she really *was* strapped for cash?

"I don't need much," she said, leaning forward expectantly in her chair. "Just a little something to tide me over until I get paid for the shampoo commercial I did last month."

His gaze fell across the family portrait on his desk. He had taken a few at Demetri and Angela's extravagant engagement party in Chicago last summer. His parents had raised him to be compassionate, to show kindness to others. So he felt compelled to help Cicely one last time. His mind made up, he grabbed his checkbook and flipped it open.

"I have an audition on Friday for a romantic comedy that begins filming at the end of the year. I'm super excited." Pride filled her eyes and brightened her face. "This could be the big break I've been waiting for *and* a huge payday, too."

"This is a onetime gift, so use it wisely," Rafael said, offering the check.

Cicely plucked it out of his hand. Her eyes darkened and the smile slid off her face. "Five thousand dollars? That's it? I was expecting six zeroes, not four."

"Of course you were. You're never satisfied, and nothing is ever good enough for you."

Cicely rubbed her hands over her stomach, slowly stroking her belly, and Rafael watched her with growing interest. He was curious about her pregnancy, couldn't help but be.

"This little one is very active today," she said, with a girlish laugh. "Give me your hand. The baby's kicking up a storm right now. It's the craziest thing."

Rafael wanted to feel the baby move, but shook his head. He didn't want to encourage Cicely's advances or make her think they were one big happy family. In fact, he wanted his ex to leave before his assistant returned from lunch. He didn't want anyone at Morretti Incorporated to know about Cicely's pregnancy, and decided it was time to end the visit. "I have to go." He rose to his feet and slammed his briefcase shut. "I'll walk you out."

"Great idea." Cicely plopped her purse on her lap, unzipped it and whipped out her oversize sunglasses. "I'm starving. How about lunch at the Four Seasons?"

"Not today." *Not ever,* he thought to himself, shrugging on his suit jacket.

"What about tomorrow?"

"I'm not available."

Cicely flinched, as if she'd been slapped, and squirmed in her chair. "Oh, no…."

Rafael grabbed his car keys off his desk and marched toward the open door. He wanted to get to the Women's Business Expo early, so he could spend a few quiet moments with Paris before she took the stage. "I don't have time for this," he said, tapping his foot impatiently. "I have somewhere important to go, so grab your things and get going."

"I can't." Cicely sniffed and raised her gaze to his eyes. "My water just broke."

Chapter 19

Paris stood on the balcony of her twelfth-floor suite at the W Hotel, clutching her BlackBerry in her sweaty palms. She couldn't help worrying about Rafael, couldn't help thinking the worst. He'd been a no-show at the Women's Business Expo yesterday and didn't even call to cancel their dinner plans. Paris was hurt that he blew her off, but tried to make light of the situation while having drinks with Cassandra at Dolce Vita Washington last night. But when Rafael didn't answer any of her calls or texts over the course of the night, panic set in. That was completely out of character for him. He was never too busy for her, always responded to her messages and called her every night before bed. *So, why hasn't he called?* she wondered, unable to calm her fears.

Every minute that ticked by felt like an hour. Her instincts told her something was wrong, that Rafael was in danger. And she couldn't shake the feeling. *Has he been in a car accident? Was he seriously injured? Is that why he hasn't returned my calls?*

Memories flooded her mind, but Paris pushed them away. She had to stay positive, had to keep the faith. Just because her mom and her fiancé both died unexpectedly didn't mean her college sweetheart had suffered the same fate.

Paris hit Rafael's contact number in her phone and prayed this time he would pick up. But he didn't. The call went straight to voice mail, and since his message box was full, she couldn't even leave a message. She tried his home number and listened with a heavy heart as his phone rang. *It's like he dropped off the face of the earth.*

Suddenly, her BlackBerry rang, but when Paris saw her father's number on the screen, her heart filled with despair. She didn't feel like talking to her dad, not when she was worried sick about the man she loved. She made a mental note to touch base with her father after she tracked Rafael down. "There must be something I can do," she said aloud.

Paris considered calling both hospitals and police stations in the area, but thought better of it. She couldn't take the risk. Rafael was one of the most successful businessmen in the country—and a millionaire bachelor who cherished his privacy and hated the paparazzi—and if the press ever got wind of a possible story they'd have a field day.

Ice spread through her veins and a cold sweat drenched her skin. Her vision blurred and a cry escaped her lips. Tears splashed onto her cheeks like raindrops. Thoughts of Rafael and all the good times they'd shared bombarded her mind. Haunted by images of him—feeding her strawberries, massaging her feet and cradling her in his arms—she struggled to control her emotions. She hadn't seen him in twenty-four hours, but it felt like weeks since she'd heard his voice and felt his tender caress.

Their last conversation played in her mind. Remembering how they'd laughed and joked and teased each other on the phone yesterday afternoon brought a sad smile to her lips.

"Wear your red Chanel suit," he'd said smoothly. "And leave your panties at home."

Paris looked at the sky, staring aimlessly at the thick, fluffy clouds. It was another windy, overcast day, and the bleak weather mirrored her crummy mood. Her eyes burned from fatigue, her bottom lip trembled, and it took all her effort not to burst into tears again. Sadness engulfed her heart and mind. Rafael had renewed her faith in love and given her hope for the future, and Paris didn't know if she could live without him. He was the man of her dreams, her soul mate, and she felt fortunate to have him in her life again. Reuniting with him in Venice had been the best thing to ever happen to her, and she thanked her lucky stars every day for bringing them back together.

Her thoughts momentarily quelled her fears, and that sickening ache in the pit of her stomach subsided. *I have to do something,* she decided, wiping her eyes with the sleeve of her robe. Paris marched back inside her suite and locked the balcony doors. No more sitting around twiddling her thumbs. She was going down to Morretti Incorporated, and she wasn't leaving until Rafael's assistant answered all her questions.

Someone banged on the door, interrupting her plan. Palms wet, her heart beating wildly, she raced through the sitting area. *God, please let it be Rafael,* she pleaded. *Please.*

Paris yanked open the door, saw her father standing in the hallway and strangled a groan. He glared at her and she glared back. Paris knew her hair and clothes were a mess, but she didn't care about her disheveled appearance. She'd lain in bed for hours last night thinking about Rafael, so anxious and afraid she couldn't sleep, and by the time the sun peeked over the horizon she was in the kitchen making coffee. Paris was determined to find Rafael, but first she had to get rid of her father.

"I told you this would happen, but you just wouldn't listen." He marched inside her suite and slammed his briefcase down on table. "I hope you're happy. Thanks to you, I'm the laughingstock of the Washington Country Club."

"What's the matter?" she asked, wondering what he was ranting about. It didn't take much to set him off—a tardy client, slow-moving lines at the bank, rain—but Paris didn't have time to listen to his grievances. Not today. "Why are you so upset?"

A frown wrinkled his face. "You don't know?"

"I don't know what?"

"You've gotten yourself into a fine mess...." Mumbling, he snapped his briefcase open and scooped up a stack of newspapers. "Baby Makes Three for Morretti Millionaire!" he read, then flung the paper clear across the floor. "Shipping Heir Delivers his Own Baby! Morretti Secret Love Child! Wedding Bells for Washington Bachelor..."

The room flipped upside down and the walls closed in around her. *That's impossible. It can't be. Rafael loves me and* only *me....* Paris couldn't breathe, couldn't think straight. Her thoughts were jumbled and nothing made sense.

Bending down, she picked up one of the discarded newspapers and stared at the bold black headline. *Baby Makes Three for Morretti Millionaire...* Her stomach heaved and her heart lurched inside her chest. The story was shocking, impossible to believe. As she read the article a headache pulsed in her temples. Her mouth dried, and for the second time in minutes, tears pricked the backs of her eyes.

Realization dawned, and suddenly everything made sense. *Rafael didn't come to the Women's Business Expo yesterday because he was with Cicely and the baby—his baby, the child I knew nothing about.* A crippling pain stabbed Paris's heart. Choking back a sob, she willed herself not to break down in front of her father. Her knees buckled under the weight of her sadness, and she dropped down onto the couch when her legs gave way.

How could Rafael be dating me and Cicely at the same time? There are only twenty-fours in a day, and when he's not at work, he's with me. They spent every available moment together, and Rafael treated her like his number one priority, as if their relationship was all that mattered. That's what made his deception all the more shocking. *Rafael's a lying, cheating snake, just like my ex. I'm better off without him.*

"We need to release a statement to the press." Her father glanced at his gold wristwatch. "You can write something up in the limo on the way to the airport."

"The airport?" Paris raised an eyebrow. "Where are we going?"

"To Atlanta, of course."

"Seriously?"

Mr. St. Clair nodded his head. "I want to spend some time with my grandkids, and if Kennedy and Anthony will have me I'd like to attend their anniversary celebration, as well."

"Dad, I'm glad to hear you say that. That's great news," Paris said, mustering a weak smile. "They're going to be thrilled to see you. I wouldn't be surprised if Kennedy bursts into tears. She talks tough but deep down she'll always be your little girl."

"Really?" Hope sparkled in his eyes. "Even though I haven't been a good father?"

"Your heart is in the right place, and that's all that matters."

Mr. St. Clair crossed the room and sat beside Paris on the couch. "I took the rest of the month off work, and I rescheduled the charity gala, as well. It was the right thing to do."

His announcement blew her mind. Paris was shocked by the news, and for a split second thought he was pulling her leg. Her father lived and breathed work, often slept in his office and hadn't taken a day off in years. "When did you have a change of heart?"

He sent her a wry smile. "After you walked out on me."

Feeling ashamed, Paris cast her gaze to the floor and fiddled with the belt on her robe.

"I gave some serious thought to what you said," he confessed, his tone solemn. "I didn't want to admit it, not even to myself, but you were right. If your mother were alive she'd be angry with how I've treated you and your brother and sister...."

Paris turned and faced her father. Talking to him helped take her mind off Rafael, and as he spoke she found herself hanging on to every word that came out of his mouth.

"I never expected to be a single father, and I screwed up a lot after your mother passed away." He blew out a deep breath and dragged a hand down his face. "When your brother dropped out of college and your sister got pregnant, I lost it. I didn't want you to go down the wrong road. So I shipped you off to Spelman and purposely isolated you from them."

They sat in silence for a moment, listening to the distant sound of morning rush-hour traffic.

"Dad, I'm not a nineteen-year-old girl anymore," Paris said softly. "I'm a grown woman, and you have to start treating me as such. I have my own hopes and dreams for the future—"

"I know. That's why I made you my second in command." Mr. St. Clair gave her a one-arm hug. "When I retire in a few years, Excel Construction will be yours. I'm expecting you to take the company to the next level."

"I don't want to be a senior executive for the rest of my life. I want to start a beauty salon franchise." The truth fell easily from her mouth, shocking them both. But as she spoke, her confidence grew and her fears dissipated.

"Why? You opened a shop several years back, and it failed miserably, remember?"

How can I forget when you keep reminding me?

"It's too risky, and besides, doing beauty treatments is

beneath you. You're a college graduate with a great mind for business. Not a lowly nail technician."

"But I love doing it," she argued. "I'm damn good at it, too."

"What makes you think this time around will be different?"

His tone was filled with doubt, but Paris didn't let his response dampen her spirits. It was time to spread her wings, to live her passion, and she refused to let anyone—even her father—kill her dreams. She believed in herself. "I'm older and wiser now, and I have twelve years of management experience under my belt." Paris lifted her chin, meeting his gaze head-on. "I have what it takes to be a success."

Mr. St. Clair stroked his chin reflectively. After several moments he slowly nodded. "Send me your business proposal, and I'll look it over next week."

"Really?" Paris raised an eyebrow and dropped a hand on her hip. "Who are you and what have you done with my father?"

Throwing his head back, he laughed long and hard. "I'm always looking for exciting new ventures to invest in, and if you have a well-thought-out plan, I'll be your first backer."

"Thanks, Dad. I really appreciate your support."

Paris settled back into the cushions. Her gaze fell on *The Washington Post* and she again zeroed in on the salacious headline. She wanted to call Stefano to find out if he'd heard from Rafael but knew better than to do so when her dad was around. For the first time in years they were having an honest-to-goodness talk. She wouldn't dare ruin the moment.

"The charity gala has been rescheduled for June, and I want the entire family to be there." Mr. St. Clair patted her hands. "It's a big night for Excel Construction and the

Soldiers' Angels organization, and I want us to present a strong, united front."

"Speaking of family, I would like you to consider hiring Anthony to work in our IT department. He's a hard worker with a wealth of experience, and I think he would be a great asset to our Atlanta office."

"Good idea. I'll discuss it with him this weekend."

Mr. St. Clair stood and pulled his cell phone out of his suit jacket. "You better get cleaned up. Our flight leaves at noon and it's almost nine o'clock."

Paris didn't know what to do. She was supposed to fly to Miami with Rafael first thing tomorrow morning. But now that he had Cicely and the— Paris's mind tripped over the word *baby,* and tears stung her eyes once again. She had believed with all her heart, with every fiber of her being, that her old college sweetheart was The One. Rafael understood her, knew her inside and out and brought out the very best in her. Paris often dreamed of them being together forever. *But how...when he has a new family?*

Deep in thought, she failed to hear the door open, but when a spicy, piquant scent of cologne filled the air, her eyes widened in surprise. *Rafael!* She glanced over her shoulder, spotting him standing beside the end table, and blinked back tears. Relief flowed through her body, and all the stress and tension of the past twenty-four hours evaporated into thin air.

Paris stared at him, studying his face. Dark circles lined his eyes, and stubble covered his chin. His blue dress shirt was open at the collar, the sleeves were rolled up and his black pants were creased with wrinkles. He looked weary, as if he'd just gone twelve rounds in a boxing match. Paris wanted to wrap him in her arms, but stayed put on the couch. He'd lied to her about his relationship with Cicely, and she didn't know if she could ever forgive him.

"Good morning," Rafael said quietly. "I apologize for interrupting."

Curses quickly fell from Mr. St. Clair's lips. "You have some nerve, showing your face here."

"I understand your anger, sir, but this is a private matter between me and—"

"Like hell it is," he seethed. "I won't let you humiliate my daughter again."

"Paris, please let me explain. The situation is not what you think."

Her father snarled like a pit bull. "Save it. She has nothing to say to you."

Rafael stared at her, pleading with his eyes. "Paris, is that true?"

Yes... No... I don't know! I'm angry and confused, and I don't know what to think anymore. You promised not to hurt me, Rafael, but you have!

"You have no business being here," Mr. St. Clair said. "Go back to your baby's mother."

"I came here to speak to Paris, and I'm not leaving until I do."

"Keep dreaming, Morretti!" Paris's father marched to the door, yanked it open and pointed outside. "Get out before I toss you out."

Chapter 20

The silence was deafening, loud enough to shatter Paris's eardrums. Conflicting feelings flooded her heart, but the strongest emotion she felt was love. It consumed her, conquered her anger. Despite everything that had happened yesterday, she still loved Rafael and didn't want her father to physically hurt him. And it was obvious he wanted to.

"Dad, can you give us a moment alone?" Paris asked, rising to her feet. "Please?"

Mr. St. Clair wrinkled his nose.

"All I need is a few minutes."

"We have a flight to catch at noon."

Seconds dragged by. Paris knew her father was disappointed in her, but she needed to hear what Rafael had to say. However, once he answered her questions he'd be out of her suite *and* out of her life forever.

"Paris, are you sure about this?"

"Yes." To convince him, she squeezed his forearm and faked a confident smile. "Dad, don't worry about me. I know what I'm doing."

Resigned, Mr. St. Clair threw his hands up in the air. "Fine, have it your way."

Relieved that he and Rafael wouldn't be trading blows, Paris sighed in relief.

"I'll be back at nine-thirty." Mr. St. Clair returned to the desk and grabbed his briefcase. "If you need me for anything…" he paused and studied Rafael "…just call. I'll be in the hotel restaurant."

"Thanks, Dad."

"Remember what I said."

Paris gave a solemn nod. "I will."

"Don't let him pull the wool over your eyes," he warned, wagging a finger in her face. "He's a liar, just like Winston. You're better off without him."

Was it true? Was Rafael cut from the same cloth as her heartless ex-boyfriend?

Her dad stalked out of the suite and slammed the door with such force the balcony doors rattled.

Paris wrung her hands, nervously shifting her feet, looking everywhere but at Rafael. They'd made love dozens of times, and she often sashayed around his Georgetown home naked, but she suddenly felt uncomfortable in his presence. *This isn't how things are supposed to be,* she thought sadly, feeling her eyes sting and burn. *We should be in the kitchen, feeding each other breakfast, not on the verge of breaking up.*

"Where are you going?"

Paris chanced a look at him, trying to make sense of his question.

"Your dad said you have a flight to catch at noon." He coughed and slid his hands into the pockets of his dress pants. "Where are you guys going?"

"That's none of your business."

His eyes narrowed, and his lips hardened into a line. Stunned by his expression, she glared at him. *He has nothing to be angry about. I'm the one who's been publicly humiliated, not him!*

"We're flying to Miami tomorrow morning on the Morretti family jet. Did you forget?" he asked.

"Take Cicely and the baby with you," she snapped, raising her voice.

He grimaced and swallowed hard.

"I'm not interested in meeting your parents—"

"But we've been planning this for weeks," he argued, interrupting her.

"That was *before* I found out about your baby mama. Now that I know you're a lying bastard, we're through." Pausing to catch her breath, Paris took a moment to gather her thoughts. She wanted to hurt Rafael, to get back at him for deceiving her, but she just couldn't do it. He was a remarkable man, the kind of person she'd always envisioned herself marrying, and she loved him. More than she'd ever loved anyone.

"Paris, I'm sorry."

"For what?" she challenged, her voice rising to dangerous heights. "For lying to me all these weeks, or for neglecting to mention that you were having a baby with your ex?"

"Hear me out."

"Why should I? We're over, and I don't want anything more to do with you."

His face fell. "You don't mean that."

"Yes, I do."

Rafael stepped forward, his hands outstretched, but Paris spurned his advances. "Don't touch me." Backing away from him, she slid behind the sofa and folded her arms across her chest. Deep down, she longed to touch him, to kiss his cheeks and lips, but knew it would be a mistake to act on her feelings. If she did, they'd end up making love, and Paris wanted to get to the bottom of things. "I was worried sick about you," she confessed, shouting her words. "I must have called you a hundred times, but you never picked up!"

"I know, and I'm sorry. My cell phone died while I was at the hospital."

"Likely story," she mumbled.

"I wanted to call and explain what was going on, but I never got a chance. Things were crazy in the delivery room, and I didn't want to leave Cicely...."

Paris winced.

"When I finally left the hospital, I came straight here."

"Is that supposed to make me feel better? Am I supposed to forget how you deceived me?" Hearing a knock on the door, she broke off speaking and glanced at the wall clock hanging above the entertainment unit. Her dad had obviously had enough of waiting, but Paris didn't mind the interruption. Listening to Rafael talk about Cicely hurt like hell, and she feared if the conversation continued she'd end up getting physically sick.

"Hotel security! Open up!"

Rafael marched over to the door and yanked it open. A short, stocky man wearing a navy blue uniform peered inside.

"Is everything okay?" he asked, his gaze scoping out the elegant surroundings.

She nodded. "Yes, of course."

"Someone overheard loud voices coming from this suite and rang the front desk. The caller feared the female occupant might be in danger." The security guard dropped his voice to a whisper. "Ma'am, are you all right?"

Paris felt her cheeks flush with heat, and she smiled apologetically. "I'm sorry for disrupting the other guests. I assure you it won't happen again." To make amends, she unzipped her purse and took a fifty-dollar bill out of her wallet. "Here is something for your trouble."

"Thank you, ma'am." He straightened his shirt and gave a curt nod. "Enjoy the rest of the day, and if you need anything don't hesitate to call the front desk."

Could this day go any worse? she wondered, turning away from the door. Feeling dejected, as if the universe was out to get her, Paris considered the events of the past twenty-four hours and decided it was the worst day of her life.

"I know you're upset," Rafael said. "But I never meant for any of this to happen."

"Then why didn't you tell me your ex-girlfriend was pregnant?"

"Because I didn't know."

Paris rolled her eyes to the ceiling.

"I'm telling you the truth. I swear."

"How could you not know? Wasn't it obvious?"

"Cicely splits her time between Washington and New York. And after she gave that tell-all interview to *Celebrity Scoop* magazine I cut all ties with her." Rafael sat down on the couch. He looked defeated, as if he didn't have any fight left in him. "Before yesterday I hadn't seen or talked to Cicely in months, and that has suited me just fine."

Paris's curiosity rose. "What happened yesterday? Why was Cicely at Morretti Incorporated? Is it true you delivered the baby in your office?"

"The story's not as exciting as the media makes it sound…."

Rafael spoke in a soft, measured tone as he recounted what had happened twenty-four hours earlier. Paris found herself enthralled, caught up in the excitement and drama of his tale. He told her about Cicely's unexpected visit, her jaw-dropping pregnancy announcement and the pandemonium that had ensued once her water broke.

"All I did was call 911," he explained with a dismissive shrug. "The paramedics arrived in less than five minutes, and I wisely stepped aside."

"How are Cicely and the baby doing?"

"Noah had the umbilical cord wrapped around his neck…."

Rafael's voice broke, and Paris rushed to his side. She wanted to comfort him, the way he'd comforted her so many times before. She clasped his hand as she sat beside him on the couch.

"It was touch and go for a while, but the doctors are confident he'll pull through." Sadness flickered across Rafael's face. "He's a little wee thing, only five pounds, so they're keeping a close eye on him in the NICU."

Paris weighed the truth of his words, giving serious thought to what he'd said. She believed him, and as much as she didn't want to admit it, he'd done the right thing yesterday. But it didn't surprise her. Rafael was an upstanding guy who put others first, and she loved him all the more for being a kind, compassionate soul. Paris heard her cell phone ring, but ignored it. She wasn't ready to leave his side, not yet. "I hope that everything works out for you, Cicely and the baby," she said quietly. "You deserve to be happy, and I wish you nothing but the best."

"Don't talk like that. My future is with you, and I want us to—"

"Rafael, there is no us. I don't do secret babies or baby mama drama. And it sounds like your ex-girlfriend is obsessed with you."

"I had a DNA test done this morning but the results won't change a damn thing." Rafael clasped Paris's hands, holding them tight. "You're the only woman I want. My feelings for you are stronger than they've ever been."

Paris felt her heart swoon inside her chest and excitement dance along her spine. His words gave her a rush, set her heart ablaze with passion and desire, but she wisely bit her tongue. She had to know where they stood or if the article she'd read that morning in *The Washington Post* was true. "Are you planning to marry Cicely so the baby can have the Morretti name?"

"The only woman I'd ever want to carry my last name is you." Gazing at her, Rafael cupped her chin gently in his palm. "Paris, I won't let you walk out of my life again. The last time almost killed me...."

Bowled over by his confession, she stared at him in stunned disbelief. Paris wanted to tell Rafael everything that was in her heart, but she didn't know where to start. He had opened up to her, freely sharing his thoughts and feelings. Paris felt closer to him than she ever had before. The more he talked, the less she worried about their future. What he said touched her deeply, and it took all her effort not to burst into tears.

"Two nights ago, while making love, you said you loved me."

Paris felt her eyes widen and embarrassment stain her cheeks. She remembered losing control of her mouth, remembered pouring out her heart and soul as she'd climaxed for the second time. But she faked amnesia now. "I did?"

"Yes, it was one of the happiest moments of my life."

His soft words were enough to make Paris cry.

"You're not wearing your diamond ring," he noted, tenderly stroking her fingers.

"I decided to sell it and donate the money to Soldiers' Angels."

Rafael cracked a smile. "That's the best news I've heard all day."

"I knew you'd say that!" she said, laughing.

"I love you, and only you," he whispered, placing light, tender kisses across her cheeks, nose and lips. "We're destined to be together. You know that, right?"

Paris nodded and raised her eyes to his face. They had lots of obstacles to contend with, but she was confident they could overcome every hurdle. Her heart guided her to tell him the truth, and tears spilled down her cheeks as she spoke. "I love you, too, Rafael, more than you will ever know, and I don't want to live without you."

"Good," he said with a chuckle. "Because I'm not going anywhere."

He kissed her then, slowly, thoughtfully, like a man hopelessly and desperately in love.

Chapter 21

Rafael opened the hood of the stainless-steel grill, doused the rib-eye steaks with his secret barbecue sauce and flipped them over. The outdoor kitchen at Nicco's Coral Gables mansion felt hotter than a furnace but Rafael was having fun making lunch.

Blowing out a deep breath, he cleaned the sweat from his brow with the back of his cooking mitts. Rafael loved being at Nicco's lavish estate, and for the second time that day considered extending his trip.

The breeze ruffled the palm trees dotting the expansive estate, birds chirped and squawked, and the intoxicating scent drifting over from the botanical garden made Rafael think about his beautiful lady. It was another sunny day in Miami, a scorching ninety-five degrees and rising, and humid. Yet Rafael didn't mind the heat.

Hell, the hotter the better.

The record-breaking temperatures had brought out the inner vixen in Paris, and since arriving in Miami they'd taken their relationship to lusty new heights. They'd made love everywhere—in the pool, in the rental car, in the VIP room of her favorite downtown nightclub. The more spontaneous they were, the hotter the fire burned.

His chest filled with pride. It always did when he thought about his girlfriend and their passionate, red-hot relationship. Paris made life interesting, and kept him guessing in the bedroom, and never failed to make him laugh. They were closer than ever, had a rock-solid bond and were committed to making their long-distance relationship work. There was no question in his mind that Paris was the only woman for him, and now that Cicely had permanently relocated to Los Angeles, he didn't have to worry about her causing problems. The DNA test had proved that he wasn't the father of baby Noah, and these days he was happier than ever. Weeks earlier, he'd accompanied Paris to her sister's anniversary party, and she'd proudly introduced him to her family and friends.

If he could now find out a way to win over Paris's father, life would be perfect. He'd visited Excel Construction several times but the businessman still hadn't warmed up to him. Rafael hoped he came around soon because he needed Mr. St. Clair's blessing before he popped the question to his daughter.

His smile widened. The big day was fast approaching, and he couldn't be more excited. With Paris's birthday only weeks away, he was more confident than ever that she would accept his marriage proposal. *What if she doesn't?* his inner voice asked, vocalizing his deepest fear. *What if Paris rejects you in front of all your friends and family? What then?*

"Then I'll keep asking her until she says yes."

Feeling a hand on his shoulder, Rafael dropped his head to his chest. Nicco and Demetri stood on each side of him exchanging bewildered looks. "Bro, you have to quit talking to yourself," Nicco said, his tone stern. "It's creeping me out."

Rafael chuckled. "My bad. I was just thinking out loud." He shrugged, wearing a sheepish smile. "You guys are in love. You know how it is."

"We sure do!" they answered in unison.

Demetri spread a crisp white cloth over the patio table and set a vase filled with long-stemmed red roses in the middle. "Angela has me wrapped around her finger, and I can't do a damn thing about it," he confessed. "Last week she forced me to watch the *Dating in the City* marathon and now I'm hooked. Nelson Hamilton is a smooth, charismatic dude. Just like me!"

Laughter flowed across the spacious backyard.

"I just realized something." Wearing a pensive expression, Nicco slowly stroked his jaw. "This time last year we were all bachelors, and now we're all in serious relationships with feisty, headstrong women."

"I know. Crazy, huh?" Demetri shook his head. "If I didn't know better I'd think Mom had something to do with it, because she's the most determined woman I know. What Vivica Morretti wants, she gets!"

"I was just thinking the same thing," Nicco said. "I wonder how she pulled it off…."

Rafael burst out laughing. His family was in Miami for the weekend to celebrate Nicco's thirty-fifth birthday and for the first time ever, they'd all have a significant other with them. His mother was good, but not *that* good. He enjoyed listening to his brothers' outrageous conspiracy theories, however.

"Shoot!" Nicco snapped his fingers. "I forgot to get the merlot from the wine cellar."

"Since you're going back inside, grab the garlic chicken for me." Rafael picked up a bottle and took a swig of his beer. "It's in the glass container at the bottom of the fridge."

"And bring me another beer," Demetri called over his shoulder. "But hurry. I'm dying out here! This heat is insane!"

Rafael turned his attention back to the grill. He finished the steaks, while Demetri chopped the vegetables and prepped the appetizers.

"Are you nervous about Paris finally meeting Mom and Dad tonight?"

Rafael shook his head. "Not at all," he said, lowering the temperature on the gas grill. "Paris is a dynamic woman with an amazing personality, and I'm confident they'll hit it off."

"I'm glad you guys reunited in Venice. You two make a fantastic couple. It's obvious Paris loves you very much."

And I love her even more. I'm finally living the American dream, and I can't wait to mak Paris my lawfully wedded wife.

"Damn, what's taking Nicco so long?" Demetri opened the oven and slid the garlic bread inside. "This is what I get for sending a boy to do a man's job!"

"Watch the steaks. I'll be right back." Rafael leveled a finger at his brother. "If they burn, I'm going to kick your ass and post the video on YouTube."

Despite himself, Demetri chuckled. "You guys are never going to let me live that video down, are you?"

"Nope," Rafael said, struggling to keep a straight face. "It's not every day we get to see a woman ream you out, and Angela gave it to you *real* good that day!"

Rafael entered the house and headed straight for the fridge. Opening it, he took out the glass container, another bottle of his secret barbecue sauce and an ice-cold beer. Realizing Nicco probably needed a hand carrying the wine bottles up from the cellar, he left the items on the counter, and jogged upstairs to the second floor.

"I lost everything because of you!"

His blood ran cold. Cranking his head to the right, he listened intently for a moment.

"You wouldn't be shit without me. *I* put Dolce Vita on the map. Not you."

A suffocating knot formed in the pit of his stomach. Rafael slumped against the wall and pressed his eyes shut. He recognized the man's voice instantly. It was Tye Caldwell, Nicco's former business partner. They used to be thick as thieves but everything changed when Nicco discovered Tye had embezzled hundreds of thousands of dollars from Dolce Vita. Instead of pressing criminal charges, Nicco had fired Tye, and the last they'd heard he was backpacking through Europe.

Light bulbs went off in Rafael's head. His instincts had been wrong. Gracie and her ex-con brother weren't responsible for the vandalism of Dolce Vita Miami, the shooting at the Beach Bentley Hotel or the brazen arson attack at Jariah's condominium complex. Tye was.

Rafael's fear escalated. He took a deep breath and with great effort squelched the panic rising inside him. Shocked and appalled by the hateful words coming out of Tye's mouth, Rafael considered the best course of action. He had a minute, maybe two, before Demetri came into the house in search of his beer and his brothers, but Rafael had even bigger things to worry about. Angela, Jariah and Paris were out shopping at Aventura Mall and would be back home any minute. But what would happen if his parents arrived first? Rafael shuddered at the thought. His father disliked Tye, always had, and the feeling was definitely mutual.

"You couldn't stand to see me succeed," Tye snarled. "That's why you forced me out of Dolce Vita. You were jealous because the spotlight was finally shining on me."

"I fired you because you embezzled money from our business and set me up to take the fall."

"Shut up! Just shut the hell up!"

Rafael inched down the hall and peeked inside the bright, spacious wine cellar. He blinked rapidly, trying to make sense of what he was seeing. He was hallucinating, had to be. Rafael rubbed his eyes and shook his head but the terrifying image still remained. Tye was pointing a black Beretta pistol at Nicco's chest, and his eyes were dark with rage.

Guilt troubled Rafael's conscience. *This is all my fault!*

The guy who'd bumped into him near his uncle's jewelry store *was* Tye Caldwell, and if Rafael had remembered to call his security team Tye would be in jail, not pointing a gun at Nicco.

In that moment, Rafael realized just how precious life was and decided that if he survived this ordeal he would propose to Paris sooner rather than later. He couldn't wait three weeks for her thirty-sixth birthday. He had her diamond engagement ring hidden in the secret compartment of his briefcase, and he'd memorized his speech weeks ago. He was ready to pop the question and couldn't think of anything better than— The thought froze in his mind and his mouth dried.

"You'd be nothing without me!" Tye raged, his tone thick with hate. "Dolce Vita was my brainchild, not yours. I poured my sweat, blood and tears into the business."

Rafael glanced around, searched for something, anything, to use as a weapon, but came up empty. He had to act now. Couldn't risk putting the people he loved in harm's way.

I don't need a weapon, I have the element of surprise on my side, he reasoned. Eyes narrowed in determination, hands balled into fists, he burst into the room and lunged at Tye. Rafael knocked him to the ground, and the gun went off. Bullets ricocheted around the room, blasted off the walls and shelves. Wine bottles shattered into a million pieces, oil paintings crashed to the floor, and the stench of gun powder polluted the air.

Anger and rage infected every inch of his body. Rafael punched Tye in the face, throwing so many blows he lost count. His hands throbbed in pain, but he didn't stop. He had to protect his family, had to save the people he loved most, no matter what.

"Bro, stop, that's enough!" Nicco grabbed Rafael's forearm and pulled him off Tye. "Damn, you knocked him out cold with one punch."

"He got what he deserved." Disgusted, Rafael stared down at Tye. He was sprawled on the floor, unconscious. His eye was swollen shut, his mouth was bloody and his white polo shirt was ripped. Broken glass littered the floor, wine flowed like the Red Sea and the air smelled sweet. "No one messes with my family and gets away with it."

"You saved my life."

"Of course I did. That's my job. I'm your big brother."

"When you burst into the room, I thought I was dreaming!" Nicco confessed with a chuckle. "When did you become such a badass?"

Rafael knew his brother was trying to make light of the situation, but he saw the pain in his eyes, heard the strain in his voice. He lobbed an arm around his hunched shoulders to let him know everything was going to be okay. Rafael heard police sirens wailing and knew help was on the way. *Demetri must have heard the gunshots and called the police.*

Expelling a deep breath didn't calm Rafael's nerves, didn't erase the violent images in his mind. His clothes were torn and bloody, but the nightmare was finally over. Everything he held dear was still safe and secure, and that was all that mattered.

Chapter 22

Rafael wasn't kidding when he said his extended family was large and boisterous, Paris thought, glancing around the dining room at Dolce Vita Miami. She'd never seen so many tall, dark and handsome men in one place, and marveled at how attractive Rafael's cousins were.

The past twenty-four hours were a blur, the scariest of her life, and as she stood at the bar listening to Jariah and Angela discuss the bridal showcase they'd attended weeks earlier, Paris found her thoughts wandering. *I can't believe Rafael took on a crazed gunman by himself. What was he thinking?*

She raised her cocktail glass to her lips and sipped her Shirley Temple. Yesterday, after a fun-filled day of shopping with Jariah and Angela, she'd returned to Nicco's Coral Gables home to find police cruisers, ambulances and news trucks parked in the driveway. Minutes later in the kitchen, Rafael and Nicco had recounted their terrifying ordeal with Tye Caldwell.

Mr. and Mrs. Morretti had arrived a little past noon, and after several rounds of hugs and kisses, they'd decided to release a statement to the press. Since there was significant damage to the second floor of the estate, Mr. Morretti had called his nephew, Realtor to the stars Dante Morretti, and arranged to rent a six-bedroom waterfront mansion for the rest of the month.

"Paris, are you okay?" Jariah asked, squeezing her forearm. "You look upset."

"I'm fine. Just overwhelmed by everything that happened yesterday."

Angela wore a sympathetic smile. "That's understandable. The past twenty-four hours have been incredibly stressful, and the media attention on Rafael has been insane."

You can say that again, she thought, expelling a deep breath. For the second time in weeks, Rafael had ended up on the front of the local newspapers. The headlines flashed in her mind, one after another. Shipping Heir Saves the Day! Morretti Family Under Attack! Gun Shootout in Coral Gables! The media was intrusive and unwelcomed. Ever since the story broke the paparazzi had been camped out at Nicco's estate. Armed bodyguards built like WWE wrestlers were stationed at the entrance of Dolce Vita. Several undercover police officers were among the crowd. Arturo didn't want anyone to ruin Nicco's birthday celebration and had taken every measure to ensure his family was safe.

"Try not to worry," Angela advised. "Things will blow over in the next couple days, and the media will move on to the next big story. They always do."

Paris glanced around the room in search of Rafael, but couldn't find him anywhere. She was still shaken up over the incident, but she put on a brave face. She didn't want to ruin the festive mood, but couldn't help feeling alone and neglected. She hadn't had a second alone with Rafael since his mother had burst into the kitchen frantically calling his name. Paris couldn't help but wonder if Mrs. Morretti was purposely trying to keep them apart.

She shook off the thought. *You're being silly,* she told herself. She had nothing to worry about, no reason to feel insecure. Later, when she was alone with Rafael, she'd share her exciting news. A smile warmed her lips. She was one step closer to opening her beauty salon, and the life she'd always dreamed of was finally within her grasp. Relocating to Washington was a big step, but Paris knew that it was the right decision. *I wonder what Rafael will say when I tell him I'm—*

"Paris, darling, may I have a word with you in private?"

Before she could respond, Mrs. Morretti took her arm and led her through the dining room. Streamers, helium balloons and ribbons hung from the ceiling. The black-and-white decor looked sharp against the colorful birthday banners. Paris heard noisemakers ring out and smiled to herself when Rafael's favorite Rod Stewart song filled the air. Tantalizing aromas wafted out of the open kitchen, and her mouth watered when a waiter rushed by carrying a silver tray topped with decadent chocolate desserts.

"Because of everything that happened yesterday we haven't had much time to talk."

Nodding, she smiled politely at Vivica Morretti, who was dressed in an ivory floor-length gown. Her glowing, caramel-brown skin was flawless and free of wrinkles.

"What are your intentions with my son?"

Paris felt her mouth sag open, and slammed it shut. "Excuse me?"

"You heard me, Ms. St. Clair." Her tone was as calm as a hypnotist's, but anger blazed in her dark brown eyes. "I want to know exactly what's going on between you and my son. Are you friends with benefits, sex buddies or a true couple?"

"With all due respect, Mrs. Morretti, our relationship is none of your business."

"You're wrong," she argued, propping a hand on her wide, full hip. "Your relationship with my son *is* my business. Rafael's my firstborn, and I won't let you or that Cicely woman play games with his heart."

"I'm nothing like that conniving gold digger—" Paris broke off when she realized she'd spoken her thoughts out loud. "I apologize. I shouldn't have said that."

To her surprise, Mrs. Morretti smiled, and her face brightened.

"Don't be," she said with a wink. "I was thinking the exact same thing!"

They both laughed, and the tension in the air lifted.

"Your son means the world to me, and I'd never do anything to hurt him." Spotting Rafael on the stage, Paris felt a heady rush of adrenaline and desire. He looked drop-dead sexy in his crisp, sky-blue shirt and white dress pants, and when their eyes met through the crowd her heart did the rumba in her chest. "Rafael is an incredible person, and I'm glad we reunited in Venice, because he's truly one in a million."

Mrs. Morretti dabbed at her eyes with her fingertips. "I was hoping you'd say that. My son adores you, and I'm glad you feel the same way."

"I do. I've loved Rafael since I was nineteen years old, and I always will."

"Welcome to the Morretti family!" Vivica threw her arms around Paris and squeezed tightly. "I think you're going to make a wonderful addition to our family, and I'm thrilled that my son found love with a strong woman *just* like his mama!"

"That's it?" Paris joked. "I was worried you were going to grill me for hours."

Vivica laughed and flapped a bejeweled hand in the air. "There's no need. I've already done three background checks on you, and you passed with flying colors!"

Rafael wasn't kidding about his mom being a gutsy spitfire, Paris thought, laughing.

A hush fell over the dining room, and the music faded to the background.

"At this time, I'd like to call my beautiful girlfriend, Paris St. Clair, to the stage."

Paris glanced over her shoulder, and gave Rafael a questioning look. *What's going on? Why is he calling me to the stage?* she wondered, resting her empty glass on the buffet table and smoothing a hand over the front of her purple, one-shoulder dress.

Paris felt hands pushing her forward, toward the small, raised stage, and laughed when Rafael's father, Arturo, appeared at her side and hustled her through the dining room. Deciding to play the role of dutiful girlfriend, she climbed the stairs and took the arm Rafael offered.

"I asked Paris to join me because I have a special announcement to make...." he said.

Me, too, she thought, concealing a smile. *And I have a feeling you're going to be thrilled! It's the most wonderful surprise ever, and I can't wait to share my good news!*

"The first time I saw you at the U of W cafeteria, I knew you were the only woman for me." Rafael gripped the microphone with one hand and caressed her cheek with the other. "I let you get away fifteen years ago, but I won't let it happen again. Reuniting with you in Venice was an act of divine intervention, and I feel fortunate to be given a second chance at true love...."

Paris heard a gasp fall from her mouth. Her vision blurred with unshed tears, and the room spun around her. She watched Rafael drop to one knee, and goose bumps pricked her clammy skin. Unspeakable joy consumed her, flowed like a river through her heart and soul. Rafael was her one true love, and the only man who'd ever really accepted her. He encouraged her to be herself, cheered her accomplishments and proved his unconditional love and support every single day.

"I love you, angel eyes, and I want to spend the rest of my life with you." Rafael reached into his pocket, took out a massive, diamond-encrusted ring and held it at the base of the fourth finger on her left hand. "Will you marry me?"

"Yes! Of course! Just say when!" Paris shouted, unable to contain her excitement. They shared a sweet kiss, one that made her heart sing. Her gaze fell to the canary-yellow, oval-shaped stunner on her left hand, and Paris decided it was the most beautiful piece of jewelry she had ever seen. "I love my engagement ring, Rafael but I love *you* even more."

Cheers, applause and whistles rose from the crowd. Light bulbs flashed, noisemakers rang out and the dimly lit dining room became boisterous and festive.

"I love you, baby. Thanks for making me the happiest man alive."

"You're welcome, and thanks for the gigantic rock!" she joked, admiring her ring.

Holding her tight, he peppered her face with kisses and tenderly stroked her hips. "We better stop before your father comes up here and beats me to a pulp. He gave me his blessing this afternoon when I met him for drinks at his hotel, but I don't want to get on his bad side..."

Rafael's words confused her, but in the crowd, just a few feet away, she spotted her family. Her dad smiled, Oliver winked and Kennedy burst into tears. Her brother-in-law flashed a thumbs-up, and Paris laughed when her nieces and nephews cheered and waved frantically. Cassandra and Stefano were standing behind her father, and seeing her best friend made Paris squeal for joy. All the people she loved and adored were in the same room, and she had her sexy new fiancé to thank. "I can't believe this," she gushed, blown away for the second time in minutes. "How did you pull this off without me knowing?"

Rafael pressed a finger to his lips. "I'll never tell."

Oh, really, she thought, hiding a smirk. *Two can play* that *game!*

"Can I have this dance?"

Basking in the glow of his love, Paris snuggled against Rafael and swayed to the beat of the soulful D'Angelo song playing in the background. Congratulations, well-wishes and cheers rang out around the dining room as guests returned to their respective tables, but Paris only had eyes for Rafael.

She tightened her hold around his waist. She felt so warm and content in his strong arms that she didn't ever want to leave. "How do you feel about a spring wedding?" she asked, nuzzling her face against his and inhaling his rich, dreamy scent. "Spring has always been my favorite time of year, and I'd love to get married right here in Miami."

Rafael raised an eyebrow. "You want to get married *this* spring?"

"Yes, of course," she said, fervently nodding her head. "How does April 5 sound?"

"That's less than two months away."

"I know, but we don't have much time."

He frowned. "We don't have much time for what?"

"What happens in Venice doesn't always stay in Venice...."

"I'm confused. You lost me." A bewildered expression crossed his face, and his scowl deepened. "What does that mean?"

Paris took his hand and placed it on her stomach. To avoid being overheard, she pressed her lips against his ear and whispered her confession. "I'm pregnant."

"You're pregnant?" he cried, his eyes wide. "How? When? I don't understand. Are you sure?"

"I'm 100 percent sure. I took four pregnancy tests this morning, and they all came out positive." Gazing up at him, she searched his face for clues about how he was feeling, but came up empty. Paris leaned in close, to feel his warmth, his support, and tenderly caressed his cheek. "I wanted to tell you after breakfast, but it wasn't the right time."

Rafael nodded, but didn't speak.

"Baby, I'm sorry. I should have told you sooner. Are you okay?"

Rafael sighed and shook his head. "I'm not okay… I'm fan-freaking-tastic!"

Paris burst out laughing and jumped into his open arms. Fifteen years after meeting, they finally had their happily ever after, and she couldn't be happier. To prove it, she kissed him passionately on the lips, for the entire world to see. Life was wonderful, better than it had ever been, and as long as Paris had Rafael, and her family by her side, she'd never want for anything.

* * * * *